DAY OF RECKONING

CODY'S WAR BOOK FOUR

STEPHEN MERTZ

WOLFPACK PUBLISHING
— EST 2013 —

WOLFPACK
PUBLISHING
— EST 2013 —

Published in the United States by Wolfpack Publishing, Las Vegas

Wolfpack Publishing
6032 Wheat Penny Avenue
Las Vegas, NV 89122

wolfpackpublishing.com

Paperback ISBN 978-1-64119-987-2
eBook ISBN 978-1-64119-988-9

Library of Congress Control Number: 2019953876

DAY OF RECKONING

PROLOGUE

Bamyan Province, Afghanistan

Once upon a distant time, Bamyan Province had been called "The Place of Shining Light". That was the literal translation of its name to English from the native Darsi language—formerly called Persian, still widely referred to as Farsi, although its name was change officially in 1964.

The Place of Shining Light. Perhaps at one time it was fitting, when the Silk Road caravans transported good between the Roman and Chinese empires, meeting in the middle to create unique classical style known as Greco-Buddhist art, but those glory days were long since gone.

Bamyan was one of thirty-four Afghan provinces, situated in the mountainous central highlands. Boasting a population of some 455,000, it was divided into six districts, administered after a fashion from the eponymous city of Bamyan, cultural capital of Afghanistan's third-largest ethnic group, the Hazara people.

Those good old days had been wiped out by fourteen hundred years of invasion and resistance, civil war and ethnic cleansing, conquest and insurgency.

Sara Durell was fluent in six languages besides her native English—Arabic, German and Russian, Cantonese and Mandarin—but she did not speak Dari or the nation's other dominant language, Pashto. For that, she'd brought along CIA linguist Roland Turmel as her interpreter and backup gunner, just in case the shit got real.

And that could happen any time.

They'd come loaded for bear, but since neither native Afghani species of *Ursus* inhabited Bamyan Province, their weapons were reserved for men.

They each carried deniable AKS-74U fully automatic carbines, manufactured by the millions since 1977 and found wherever Russians made war, feuded, or collected cash for surplus arms, no questions asked. Their backup pieces were anonymous Glock semiautomatic pistols, chambered for 9mm Parabellum rounds, used by a bewildering array of police and intelligence agencies in sixty-odd nations, including nearby Pakistan's Inter-Services Intelligence.

The mission: spy and eavesdrop on a Taliban faction preparing to surpass its parent movement's rancid record for subversion and international terrorism. Sara was hoping to come out of it alive, but just in case, they were employing high-tech gear that would record their enemies and broadcast details of their plots halfway around the world to Langley's George Bush Center for Intelligence.

The weapons standing by to wreak havoc were twofold. One was a new strain of heroin, more fiendishly addictive than the other forms of "normal" smack that circulated globally. Over sixteen years of U.S. occupation, with at least $1 trillion poured into the sand so far, Afghanistan remained the world's top producer of heroin and hashish, the land under dope cultivation expanding yearly, and this new twist would expand its foreign markets exponentially.

And now, on top of that, came rumbles of a "Devil's Rain"—a hideously deadly chemical, details remaining vague so far—that was supposed to be much worse than chlorine gas released in Syria against purported "rebels" by tyrant Bashar Assad. Afghanistan and neighboring nations were rife with ethnic and religious conflict spanning centuries, on top of which American "Crusader" troops would make prime targets for the Taliban and kindred militants.

The projected death toll: millions, if the Devil's Rain was offered to jihadists in the Middle East, and who could say where it would go from there? Reports, still unsubstantiated, claimed the Taliban had chemists working overtime on mass production, hoping they could supplement their war chest both with sales of lethal gas and their new high-test smack, posing a menace to the world at large.

Sara Durell was here, crouching in darkness with Turmel and his equipment at her side, flies on the wall as terrorists got down to business for the final stages of their scheme. She guessed that much of their discussion would involve dollars and cents—or dinars, euros, rubles, pounds sterling, whatever—along with details of delivery for customers already lining up from the Middle East to Europe, Russia, North Korea, and the vast Americas.

Job one: obtaining confirmation of the double-threat and any details that could aid with interdiction. To that end, Sara wasn't supposed to simply kill the plotters as they haggled over details, less than thirty feet away. Langley and Washington had vetoed a preemptive strike as premature, counterproductive, yada-yada.

Still, that let her with a twitchy trigger finger, wishing she could move against her enemies directly, try to nip their latest nightmare in the bud.

Her earpiece made Durell think that the meet was winding down, a judgment emphasized by sounds of shuffling feet, men rising from the pillows serving them as furniture inside the smallish house they'd targeted, one building in a rural village dominated by the Taliban. She turned to Roland, caught his nod, and raised a finger to delay uncoupling of his gear, intent on snatching every bit of conversation they could get.

With that thought foremost on her mind, she almost missed the sound of stealthy footsteps drawing near, approaching from the west, on their left flank.

She touched Turmel's arm lightly as she rose, swinging her carbine up and into readiness as Roland palmed his microphone and started rising to his feet.

Too late.

The roving lookout shouted something Sara couldn't translate but still easily interpreted by tone and volume. In the house, she didn't need a techno-ear to pick up sounds of frightened men scrambling for any exit readily available, and then the sentry cut loose with a burst from his Kalashnikov.

In front of Sara, inadvertently blocking her field of fire, Turmel let out a grunt of pain and landed at her feet. He didn't twitch around or make noise like a wounded man, and Sara guessed that he was dead before he'd hit the ground. Her burst of 5.45mm rounds repaid the sentry, dropped him in a heap before she crouched and felt for Roland's pulse.

Found none.

More troops were on the way as Sara grabbed Turmel's recorder and secured it, sprinting into darkness with no time to make it stealthy. Automatic weapons tracked her, but they hadn't loaded tracers, and the moonless desert night conspired to help her getaway.

She fled without a backward glance or second thought. Forget the propaganda about no man left behind. The digital recording she'd secured was worth a hundred lives, bare minimum, and nothing mattered more right now than getting clear, successfully transmitting the intelligence they'd gathered to the people who were authorized to act upon it.

Sara needed time, perhaps not much of it, to finish what she'd started in Bamyan Province.

She ran as if her life and millions more depended on it— which, in fact, they did.

CHAPTER 1

Caracas, Venezuela

Jack Cody stood in darkness on a rooftop in Valle Arriba, counting down the seconds to a fight for life.

Despite its proximity to the U.S. embassy and others, Valle Arriba ranked among the Venezuelan capital's riskiest neighborhoods, and that was saying something for Caracas overall. At last report, Caracas had the world's worst murder rate outside a war zone—120 victims per 100,000 residents—and 98 percent of all reported crimes remained unsolved.

That came as no surprise to Cody, though domestic homicides were not the issue that had brought him to what paid promoters called "The City of Eternal Spring" and "Heaven's Branch on Earth". Take any time at all to look beyond the superficial glitz, and the PR was bound to make you laugh—or maybe gag.

Aside from its astounding murder rate, accelerated by

the country's reputation as an international transshipment point for narcotics, Venezuela ranked fourth worst among twenty-three nations listed by the U.S. State Department as "Tier 3" human trafficking zones. Tier 1 included thirty-two countries in full compliance with the Trafficking Victims Protections Act of 2000. Tier 2 encompassed eighty-seven nations whose governments don't "fully comply" with the TVPA's minimum standards but are making "significant efforts" to try. Tier 3 is at the barrel's bottom, states that don't comply and make no efforts to reform.

In Venezuela, as in certain other countries, trouble started at the top and filtered down.

To Jack, that meant the current president, one Nicolás Maduro Moros. A bus driver turned union activist, he'd clawed his way up the political ladder over the past nineteen years, from the National Assembly to Minister of Foreign Affairs under President Hugo Chávez, then Vice President until a heart attack and cancer killed Chávez in March 2013. Maduro polled 51 percent of the popular vote in that year's special presidential election, after a campaign financed by two nephews-in-law smuggling cocaine into America. They'd helped him with his next election too, in 2015, before DEA agents busted them stateside in what Maduro decried as "an imperialist ambush", and Moros clung to despite protests of electoral chicanery. Allies Cuba, Russia, China and Syria stood behind him, while the U.S., Canada, and most of Western Europe backed rival Juan Guaidó as interim president.

Not that Maduro gave a damn.

In 2018 a Board of Independent Experts branded Maduro "responsible for dozens of murders, thousands of extra-judicial executions, more than 12,000 cases of arbitrary detentions, more than 290 cases of torture, attacks against the judiciary and a state-sanctioned humanitarian crisis affecting hundreds of thousands of people". In July 2017 the U.S. Treasury Department sanctioned seventeen Venezuelan officials for rigging that year's Constitutional Assembly election. Two months later, Ottawa imposed sanctions barring Canadian nationals from financial transactions in Venezuela. Both countries and Great Britain had travel advisories in effect, warning tourists to avoid the so-called "Land of Grace".

No wonder, then, that any shady deal you could imagine thrived under Maduro.

As reported by State, Venezuela filed few reports on anti-trafficking efforts, logging seven arrests but no convictions under Maduro's regime. A stringent law enacted in 2007 gathered dust, while Venezuela ranked as both a source and destination country for men, women, and children condemned to forced labor and sexual slavery. Venezuelan females of all agers, either kidnapped or lured from the boonies to urban and tourist centers, were either shipped abroad or earmarked for domestic child sex tourism on par with Thailand's. Trafficked women commonly wound up in brothels throughout the Caribbean islands, while victims from other South American nations, together with Asians, Africans and Filipinos, wound up as domestic slaves for rich Venezuelans or affluent foreigners.

Tonight, Cody was gunning for a local crew that had a high turnover in Caracas and environs, paying off Maduro's people in the Bolivarian National Police with cold cash and warm merchandise samples, ensuring that arrests were few and far between, convictions holding steady at zero.

That was about to change.

Cody was on a mission for the CIA, the only kind that he accepted since the murders of his wife and children while he was at war with strangers in the Middle East. No longer stoked on living, every breath a grim reminder of his loss, he now accepted only jobs where death stood waiting for him at the bitter end. To his mind, it was pure bad luck that he'd survived this long.

Bad luck for him, and worse luck for the human garbage on his naughty list.

He'd come prepared for anything to Valle Arriba, armed with a Steyr AUG assault rifle, a pair of Glock 22 pistols chambered for .40-caliber Smith & Wesson rounds, and four M67 fragmentation hand grenades. He planned to use the latter sparingly, bearing in mind that hostages were likely caged somewhere around the target premises.

And it was time to move.

Right now.

At thirty years of age, Eugenio Herrera reckoned he was satisfied with life so far. He had some unfulfilled ambitions, granted—chiefly rising higher than his present *teniente*'s rank within the Bolivarian National Police Directorate of Operations and Special Tactics, perhaps to command the whole force in due time—but he was happy with his wife and mistress, bribes that roughly tripled his official yearly salary, and the authority that let him do whatever he damn pleased for the most part.

Tonight, he'd been assigned to supervise a shipment from the Venezuelan hinterlands, girls and young women outward bound for cribs maintained by prostitution syndicates in Haiti, Saint Lucia, and Barbados. Altogether, forty pieces would be marched aboard a tramp steamer, *El Tiburón*, and shipped off to a fate nearly beyond imagination, which none of them would escape.

Herrera took a drag on his bitter cheroot, adjusted the Browning Hi-Power pistol on his hip, holstered beside his round gold-plated badge, and told Vassak Brachamios, "It's almost time."

Vassak was a *kryetar*—an underboss—in the Armenian Mafia, a syndicate notorious worldwide for trafficking in drugs, arms, people, even human organs. He was fat and balding, with a blotchy red complexion and a case of halitosis no mouthwash seemed strong enough to tame. Rumors suggested that he'd murdered ten to fifteen men, a tally that impressed Herrera with a mere nine executions to his own credit.

Brachamios consulted the Rolex Oyster Perpetual watch on his fat wrist and produced a huffing sound that might have been agreement or a warning sign of indigestion from the spicy *soujouk* sausage he consumed in epic quantities. Watching him eat sometimes, Herrera couldn't help but think of *Stand By Me,* the movie featuring a film-within-a-film called "The Revenge of Lard Ass Hogan".

Cristo, he could even kill Herrera's wolfish appetite.

"I guess so," Vassak slurred, nearly as poor at speaking English as he was with Spanish. "You see anything downstairs you like?"

Herrera scowled at the question, as if it were an insult. Truth be told, he'd sampled Vassak's merchandise from time to time, always using a condom to avoid disease. As his father was wont to say, *Más vale prevenir que cura.*

Better safe than sorry.

After Brachamios was on his feet, joints creaking from the weight they carried, then Herrera rose, careful to shy away from contact with the reeking mobster. Men like this were useful, their transactions within Venezuela tacitly encouraged by *El Presidente,* but that didn't mean Herrera had to like them.

He would happily accept their cash, of course, keeping his portion of it while he passed the lion's share upstairs to headquarters and on from there to politicians serving President Maduro, but they weren't his friends by any means.

In fact, he wasn't even sure they rated being classified as human beings. More like troglodytes, somewhere between chimpanzees and *medias razas* on the evolutionary scale.

If things like Vassak didn't come with cash in hand, Herrera gladly would have placed them all before a firing squad.

The captives were downstairs, as usual, confined to quarters almost as foul-smelling as Brachamios. The chamber held one hundred "comfortably", but was often overcrowded, with a single toilet no shower, no hint of privacy. On the occasions when he'd sampled Vassak's wares, Herrera had removed his chosen partner to an upstairs room outfitted with a double bed and sink for washing up, before or afterward. No windows, and he'd made damned sure there were no hidden cameras or microphones that might be used against him later for blackmail.

That would have been the final straw for Vassak and his goons, no matter how much money they poured into President Maduro's United Socialist Party. He would have dumped them in the Orinoco wetlands, food for *los caimans* if the reptiles did not find them indigestible.

Herrera made a sour face and fanned the air around him as Brachamios broke wind and laughed about it, like a stunted child in grade school. Waddling toward the exit, he reminded the lieutenant of a hog that had escaped its sty, bewildered, searching for the wallow it called home.

At least the pig amused himself, while keeping conversation to a minimum.

They'd reached a hallway, wide enough for the Armenian to pass but not much more, when an explosion rocked the building. Instantly, Herrera drew his Browning pistol, as Brachamios produced a sidearm from beneath his loose-cut *campesino* shirt. The bloated man's whole manner changed immediately, as he went on full alert.

Like the lieutenant, Vassak clearly recognized the echo of a hand grenade.

Within another second, automatic weapons started firing, their reports stinging Herrera's ears. Turning to face him, Vassak growled, "*Kanayk'!*"

"*¡Habla ingles, gordo!*" Herrera snapped, then caught himself. "Speak English, fat man!"

"The women," Brachamios translated, overlooking the insult. "We have to get them out!"

Cody preferred a soft approach to any target at the start, until he'd gained a physical advantage and the killing could no longer be postponed, but circumstances altered cases.

There was also something to be said for shock and awe.

After descending from his rooftop lookout post, he'd moved along an alley lined with pungent garbage cans to reach a loading dock behind his target. Mounted concrete steps to gain some altitude and spent a moment with his lockpicks as he cracked the hellhole's backdoor, listened briefly at the crack, then eased inside.

Light midway down a dingy corridor relieved the inner darkness, spilling from an open door along with two or three male voices, set against the background music of a band he didn't recognize by name but might have been Ghoulchapel, Armenia's takeoff on AC/DC.

Whatever. It was time to shut the party down.

Jack didn't risk a glance around the doorjamb as he neared

it, simply palmed one of his frag grenades, released its pin, and lobbed the orb inside. Retreating, crouching down, he heard a sound of the M67 bouncing on a table, toppling glass that sounded like beer bottles, then it blew, and shit got real.

Cody was wearing Mighty Plugs, crafted from beeswax to protect his eardrums from the sounds of combat. They were pliable and far superior to foam at muting sounds of shots, explosions and the like, while still allowing normal conversation to proceed.

Not that he planned on chatting with his enemies tonight.

A look inside the lounge revealed a scene of carnage, three men bleeding out from shrapnel wounds, one with his left arm hanging by raw tendons. Playing cards were scattered all around them, oversized confetti. Cody left them to it, all three losers now, and moved on down the corridor, homing on sounds as the remainder of the team in residence responded to his opening salvo.

He'd guesstimated that there were a dozen men or more inside the place, all packing heat, but taking down the card players had shaved those hostile odds by 25 percent. The rest would go down harder, but they didn't know who they were up against.

Their loss.

Down range, the far end of the hallway, a lone gunman showed himself and froze, surprised to see his enemy advancing from a drifting cloud of HE smoke and drifting plaster dust. He held a compact submachine gun—Cody couldn't say what kind, offhand, and didn't care—shouting out something in Armenian.

A warning to his friends? A call for backup from the rest? Or was he dumb enough to waste time questioning his enemy instead of getting down to business?

Either way, he'd waited too damned long.

A three-round burst from Cody's AUG stitched holes across the skinny gangster's chest and pitched him over on his back. Falling, he managed to squeeze off a burst of auto fire—9mm Parabellum by its sound—but only ripped a zigzag pattern in the ceiling's cheap acoustic panels.

Useless.

Cody reached the twitching near-corpse and discovered that he had a choice of turning left or right from there. Most of the racket emanated from his left, so he went that way, picking up his pace, ready for anything.

A voice with some authority behind it overrode the babble of excitement, shouting orders in Armenian. Translating might have helped a bit, but Jack made do with Arabic, Spanish and Russian, in addition to his native tongue.

No matter.

He could figure out what they were saying from the tone and context, variations on demands to find out what was happening, seasoned with expletives requiring no interpretation.

Panic in the air, and rage at being caught with their guard down.

Jack Cody's specialty.

Beyond his line of sight, people were cocking guns and making all the other sounds that went along with combat, when a group of lazy thugs was taken by surprise. Voices were drawing closer, all but one of them speaking Armenian, forsaking broken English *in extremis*. One, however, alternated between English and Spanish, the former spoken with a lilting Latin accent.

Venezuelan? Probably.

A trafficker or maybe something worse: a cop or politician who'd gone so far down the rabbit hole of greed that he had dropped into a cesspool of corruption.

Fair enough.

Tonight, Jack meant to pull the plug on one and all of them.

As for their captives, if he found any in residence, they would be screened by soundproof walls and doors. No point alarming nosy neighbors with their cries for help that never came.

But it was coming now.

One man committed to relieving misery—his own included, if his luck held out—had come to save the day or die trying.

Eugenio Herrera fought against a rising sense of panic, trying to decide exactly what was happening. The BNP tried to control the volatile domain of syndicated crime in Venezuela—never absolute, given the psychopathic personalities involved—but strict enough to nip most feuding in the bud and map out territories with a range of sanctions on a sliding scale from monetary fines to summary eradication.

It had worked—so far, at least—because no foreign or

domestic criminals dared to make war against the National Police, backed by 130,000 army troops, 70,000 National Guardsmen, 12,000 marines, and 20,000 BNP officers, including the agency's deadly 1,300-man Special Actions Force. No syndicate on Earth, including China's mighty Triads, dared to buck those odds.

There had been hiccups on the way, of course, even some massacres, but order was maintained today, for the most part, because the president's goodwill demanded a façade of peace.

Now, this.

Vassak Brachamios stopped short, blocking Herrera's progress, while he opened an apparent linen closet to reveal an arsenal or automatic weapons, shotguns, even pistols hanging on the backwall, pegs protruding from their trigger guards. The fat Armenian picked out an AK-47, slung a bandoleer of extra magazine over one meaty shoulder, and advised Herrera, "Take whatever pleases you."

Herrera slipped his Browning back into its holster, reaching past Brachamios—no easy task—to snatch an M4 carbine fitted with a Beta C-Mag hundred-round drum magazine. He knew the weapon's specs by heart, aware that firing on full auto would exhaust that load in less than seven seconds flat, but in the process, it would lay down an imposing screen of fire that might allow Herrera to escape.

And if he did, there would be hell to pay for the Armenians, over their lame security, and for whoever dared to violate *El Presidente*'s standing rules.

"Come on," Vassak urged him. "We have to get the merchandise away from here."

Herrera recognized the sense in that. Aside from mobsters dying—which could be explained away as just another gang war, soon to be suppressed—exposure of sex trafficking would be a PR nightmare for Maduro and his ruling party.

Would it topple the administration? Likely not, but it would give Maduro's enemies more ammunition for attacks at the United Nations and through global media.

And if that happened on Herrera's watch, he might as well start looking for a new career.

Assuming he survived the night.

As if in answer to his morbid thoughts, another high explosive blast ripped through the building, followed closely by the cries of hurt or dying men.

Vassak rushed forward, moving with a speed Herrera had not witnessed from the man before, fat wobbling beneath his clothing to impart an almost comic aspect to their stark emergency. He shouted Eastern European gibberish, a guttural barrage of words that *el teniente* could not understand, presumably exhorting his disordered troops to stand and fight.

A combination kitchen-dining room opened in front of them, its atmosphere a heady mix of frying meat and cordite, with a taint of body odor, Vassak turning toward a doorway that Herrera knew gave access onto basement stairs.

Below, they'd find another door, that one double-locked, soundproof and forced entry resistant. Behind it were the females waiting to be extricated, driven to the waterfront inside a semi's trailer, then loaded into a forty-foot cargo container for a one-way cruise to final disposition.

Would they welcome death at this point? Possibly. But it was not their choice.

As for rescue, Herrera was supposed to backstop the Armenian defense team, but he wondered now if he was up to it.

Vassak opened the seeming pantry door, revealed the staircase, and was jangling keys in preparation for descent when a strange voice addressed him, saying, "Drop your piece, Chubby, and put that keyring on the counter."

Speaking English with no trace of any accent that Herrera could identify.

He turned to find a man armed with an automatic rifle covering the two of them. Herrera recognized the weapon as a Steyr AUG and understood its capabilities. He also registered the stranger checking out the badge clipped to Herrera's belt.

"A dirty cop," the gunman said. "What will they think of next?"

Too much.

Off to his left, Herrera saw Vassak begin to raise his folding-stock Kalashnikov toward target acquisition. That was the lieutenant's cue to try his own luck with the borrowed M4 carbine, index finger tightening around its trigger as he made the irreversible decision.

Three weapons seemed to fire in unison, but the lieutenant saw his rounds tracking across the kitchen cabinets beyond his human target, high and to the left. Vassak Brachamios was coming no closer with his Kalashnikov, unloading half a magazine before the Steyr's 5.56mm rounds ripped into him with soft, wet sounds like a meat-tenderizing mallet striking flesh.

Herrera felt the impacts on his own flesh, lurching backward toward the open doorway to the basement stairs and gasping as he tumbled down them, his M4 still firing impotently, something cracking loudly in his neck as he collided with the steel door down below.

Footsteps descending now, the victor standing over him with Vassak's keys in hand. The stranger met his eyes, and just before his image faded out, he said, "You should have played it straight, *ese.*"

Jack counted twenty-seven captives in the basement, all female. Their ages visually ranged from mid-teens into early twenties, each attractive in her own way, even though they hadn't showered recently and all of them had been through Hell, with nothing else ahead of them as long as they survived as prisoners.

A few already looked as though death would come as a relief. The rest stood gaping at him in the basement doorway, AUG in hand, and expressions shifting as they recognized the dead cop huddled at his feet.

"¿Quién eres tú?" one asked him.

"¿Has venido a ayudarnos?" another queried.

And a third, maybe the youngest of the lot, demanded, "¿Estamos a salvo ahora?"

Cody raised a hand for silence, and the prisoners—cowed

by abuse in custody—stopped clamoring. He answered back, "It doesn't matter who I am, but yes, I'm here to help you. As to being safe, I need to get you out of here as soon as possible and call in the authorities."

"¡No! ¡No policía!" said a redhead in the front row, pointing toward the last man Jack had killed. "Él era un policía."

"Not Venezuelan cops," he said. "I'll get you to the US Embassy, the FBI, and we can work it out from there."

He'd be entrusting that job to a stranger—from the CIA, not from the Bureau—but Jack knew there was no point in going over that right now. The racket from his takedown of the slavers likely had neighbors dialing the BNP, even from this suspicious, rundown neighborhood.

They had to move, and Cody knew the liberated captives couldn't fit into the Honda Civic he'd been handed, with his weapons, on arrival at Simón Bolívar International Airport that morning. He'd also seen there was a semi parked outside, labeled "Sucre's Prime Meats", maybe a bit of twisted humor, scumbag slavers laughing up their sleeves at the expense of human decency.

As if they even knew the meaning of the words.

"Ven ahora," Cody urged the girls and women. "Come on, now. They've got a truck outside. I'll get you to the embassy and have guards waiting on arrival."

The same front-row redhead challenged him. "¿Cómo podemos confiar en ti?"

"How can you trust me?" Jack replied. "Lady, I just killed thirteen men to get you out of here. And think about it: who else have you got?"

The muttering died down as Cody started up the stairs, his rescued hostages in single file behind him, like a row of ducklings following their well-armed hen through territory fraught with peril. This time, though, the danger had been crushed and cast aside. They moved past crumpled bodies, through rooms splashed and sprayed with blood, all silent now.

It was a testament to what these victims had already suffered, Cody thought, that none seemed sickened by the grisly sights and smells.

Outside, in what passed for fresh air, he paused to grab his go bag from the Honda, then proceeded to the waiting truck, relieved to find its keys in the ignition so he wouldn't have to hot-wire it. The rear doors of the semi's trailer were unlatched, a padlock dangling, and he pitched it off into the night before he dragged a ramp down from inside and started loading passengers on board.

When they were all secure inside, before closing the doors, he told them, "It's about a fifteen-minute drive from here at normal speed, to keep from getting stopped be by *la policía*. Some ought to be arriving here before much longer, after all the noise I made. I'll phone ahead when we get rolling. Any questions?"

There were none, but someone at the back called out, "¡Dios te bendiga!" She got the others started, wishing him God's blessing, but Jack figured that was a lost cause, far past its sell-by date.

He closed the double doors and walked back to the semi's cab, climbed up into the driver's seat and dropped his go bag on the floor, then gunned the engine into life.

When he had put two blocks between them and the slaughterhouse, Jack took his Iridium GO! roam phone from a pocket, switched it on, and dialed the embassy's unlisted number. Modern software sent his calls around the world, bouncing from ten to fifteen servers average in seconds flat and keeping them untraceable.

A spook from Langley answered, listened to Jack's message, and assured him that U.S. Marines would greet the embassy's incoming guests upon arrival. Signing off, Jack noted that he had been forced to ditch his borrowed car in Valle Arriba, soon to be discovered by police.

"No problem, sir," the spook replied. "It's cold."

"Okay. See you in ten, or thereabouts."

"Before you go, sir…"

"What?"

"We received a message for you. Someone couldn't reach you, so they left a callback number."

"Give it to me."

Cody memorized the fourteen digits, three of them the "011" international call prefix for any place in the United States. Beyond that, Jack assumed the number was a one-time-only job, ready to disconnect for good as soon as he'd received more orders from his handler at the Company, Sara Durell.

But this time, he was wrong.

After he hung up on the embassy, Jack dialed the number that he'd never seen before. A man's voice answered midway in the gap between its first and second rings.

He recognized the voice and wasn't pleased to hear it.

Denham Boyd, Sara Durell's White House liaison, telling Jack, "You're an elusive one."

"Somebody should have told you I was working," Cody said, without apology.

"Are you clear now?"

"Five minutes, give or take. A drop-off, then I'm out of here."

"Hold on," Boyd said. "I've got some news."

And it was almost never good. "So, spit it out," Cody replied.

"It's Sara."

"What about her?"

"She's in trouble. Missing. In Afghanistan."

CHAPTER 2

"Details!" Cody demanded.

Boyd considered that for half a second, then replied, "It's need-to-know."

"Why even tell me then?"

"Jack…"

"Denham, spill it. Now."

"Bare bones, only. Is this line air-tight?"

"You know it is. Get on with it."

Another heartbeat's hesitation, then Boyd pressed ahead. "I'll just say this: We got a rumble on the Taliban from Bamyan Province. Know where that it?"

"Been there, done that," Cody said.

"Okay. Some bad shit coming down the pipeline. Worse than usual. I can't get into details with you, honestly."

"So, skip to Sara. When did she go back to field work?"

"It's a special op, with emphasis on 'special'. Going in with an interpreter to get a fix on those responsible and set them up."

Meaning a Predator with Hellfire missiles, Jack supposed. He didn't bother asking why that fell to Sara, didn't care. Just said, "I'm listening."

"She found them. Got enough on digital to make a case, then something happened. Sounded like a sentry stumbled onto them."

"When you say 'sounded like'..."

"It's on the high-speed audio she sent, along with rough coordinates."

"A pickup operation?"

"More or less," Boyd said.

"Start making sense, Denham."

"Is that—?"

"A threat?" Jack interrupted him. "Call it whatever. We can do this now, or face to face, later."

Boyd didn't try to bluff it out with any of that "you can't touch me" bullshit. He knew better, knew damned well that Cody could touch anybody if he put his mind to it.

That's one advantage of a man with nothing left to lose.

"You need to stay away from this, Jack," he advised. "I'm serious. We have good people presently en route."

"How good?"

"The best on tap. A team of Navy SEALs who've done this kind of thing before."

"With Sara?"

"No, but..."

"Skip it. I want to be in the neighborhood, in case they drop the ball."

Jack wasn't asking for permission, didn't want or need it. Thinking past the words Boyd was required to say, Cody suspected that Sara's liaison to the Oval Office wouldn't mind having a skilled backup on hand. Plan B already waiting in the wings.

"Well, if I can't stop you..."

"Take that as given," Cody said.

"Thing is, on this I can't provide connections at the other end."

"Don't need them. I still have some friends in that neck of the woods."

Or did he? Cody hoped so, but he hadn't been in touch with them since he'd received the news about his family and left the sandbox, snatching time to mourn before he shifted gears and found another war that offered him a route toward payback, coupled with an exit strategy.

If his former friends were still alive, they might not know that Jack was. He couldn't believe they would have shifted sides, but people absolutely went through changes in Afghanistan, considering their old alliances and maybe finding new ones. If his former comrades had survived this long, no word from Cody in the interim, what would they even think of him today?

Later for that.

He'd find out as he went along.

"You'll keep me posted?" Denham asked him.

"Doubtful."

"Hey, now—"

"Remember, I don't work for you."

"You want to make this personal?" asked Boyd.

"What isn't?"

"Look, we all work for The Man."

"Who's leaving it to you, apparently."

"And I'm just saying, maybe I can help you."

"*If* I go in, *if* I need help, I'll leave that call up to Sara."

"Jack, you realize—"

"Don't say it," Cody warned, and cut the link.

If Boyd was following the rules, the number he'd been calling from would be deactivated instantly, wiped out as if it never had existed in the first place. That was fine with Jack. He didn't plan on using it again, whatever happened from now on.

As he'd been promised, two marines were waiting for him at the embassy's fortified gate, dressed in combat utility uniforms, MARPAT digital camouflage under modular tactical vests, both armed with M16A2 rifles and Beretta M9 pistols on their hips. A PFC kept the semi covered, while a lance corporal came around the driver's side, eyeballing Cody.

"You're the one who called ahead, sir?"

"Roger that."

"Your cargo, sir?"

"In back, unlocked. I'll need to keep the ride."

The E-3 circled back and Cody heard the truck's backdoor creak open. Bustling movement in the cab's wing mirrors but he didn't bother watching as the hostages unloaded, passing through the gate, beyond embassy walls and hidden from the street.

What happened to them next was someone else's worry.

Jack had troubles of his own.

The trailer's door slammed shut, the E-3 thumping it and calling out, "You're good to go, sir."

Cody waved a hand in answer, shifted into gear and pulled away, using the street map in his head to chart a thirteen-mile route from the embassy on Avenida Baralt, in the capital's Federal District, to Simón Bolívar International Airport on Avenida La Armada in Maiquetía, in the state of Vargas. Guidebooks said the trip through "light traffic" should take thirteen minutes, but Jack had ample time to kill, first checking in, then flying some eight thousand miles, a twenty-hour trip not counting layovers.

Too goddamned long, but Cody's mounting rage had no effect on time or physics.

All it meant was more grief for his enemies when he arrived.

Washington, D.C.

All things considered Denham Boyd supposed his chat with Jack had gone as well as anybody could expect. He'd dropped the bomb, issued a warning not to interfere, and Cody had refused to play along.

So far, so good.

Call that Plan B.

Plan A was Boyd's personal choice, and he still hoped the Navy SEALs could pull it off. Extraction of an asset from a hot zone ranked among their varied specialties, along with taking out high-value targets like Osama bin Laden and securing forward outposts in the everlasting War on Terror, like Afghanistan's Camp Rhino.

SEALs were good, on par with Delta Force, but they weren't always winners. Mogadishu was a case in point, along with "Operation Urgent Fury" in Grenada under Reagan and Panama's "Operation Just Cause" under Bush Forty-one. Don't even *think* about his son's pursuit of those alleged Iraqi nukes.

Shit sometimes happened to the best-laid plans of men and all that jazz.

Jack Cody hadn't dropped the ball on any of his missions yet, but no one could protract that kind of lucky streak forever. On the up-side, Cody didn't seem to care if he survived or not, since psychopaths had put his wife and children in the ground.

Boyd, married only to his job, could sympathize but never actually feel the kind of Hell that Cody lived through every day. Right now, Boyd's first concern was bringing Sara Durell safely home, not only for her own sake, but for his.

Failure on that scale wouldn't win him any White House brownie points and might just land him on the unemployment line. Political ambition was a stubborn beast, but it could still be put to sleep.

Get caught with kiddie porn, for instance, or expose some indiscretion in the "Me Too" age. Maybe appear too cozy with the Kremlin, although much of that Cold War taboo had faded recently.

Losing a CIA team in Afghanistan was marginal, but there was no requirement for a scandal in the media. A presidential whim could put Boyd on the outs in Washington and farther down the line, maybe until he hit the grassroots level, managing some wishful thinker's first campaign.

Screw that.

Boyd hadn't borne the slings and arrows of outrageous fortune, yada-yada, just to see his whole career flushed down the crapper now. He'd find some way to put a decent spin on Sara's fate, whatever that turned out to be.

If he could sell it to the POTUS, he could manage anyone—except, perhaps, one wild-ass soldier with a death wish, who cared nothing for the hopes and dreams of Denham Boyd.

His cell phone buzzed softly, vibrating in his pocket. Denham whipped it out and brought its screen to life. The Man's personal secretary didn't have to sign her name. The message said it all.

UR wanted stat.

That was a medical expression meaning now, immediately, asap, so get your ass in gear. Boyd didn't like the connotation of extreme emergency, much less the implication that someone might not survive the present crisis.

It was right up there with "Code Blue" in the jargon of disaster, meaning someone's heart had stopped or they had ceased to breathe, requiring a crash team's best effort to resuscitate whoever that might be.

In this case, did that make Denham the ER doctor or the loser on a gurney?

There was only one way he could answer that, and it meant heading for the Oval Office, stat.

Keeping his fingers crossed that his career wasn't already DOA.

Bamyan Province

"What progress?" Sediq Qayoumi asked.

"None yet, sir," Ehsan Abarkhyl answered. "You have my sincere—"

"Before you say 'apologies', Ehsan, consider how little they mean to me."

"I understand."

"Results are all that matter in this world. Excuses count for nothing."

"*Nem sidi.* Every man available is searching as we speak."

"How many?" Sediq asked.

"Sir?"

"You tell me every man available is hunting for the infidel. I ask how many men?"

"Um…I believe it is approximately—"

"No. *Exactly*, Ehsan. If I want 'approximately,' I can pluck a number from my *mustaqim* as well as you can."

Qayoumi took a certain pleasure from the flush that rose in Ehsan's pitted cheeks. As district leader of the Taliban and originator of their current plan, code-named *Nihayat Ale-alam*—"Apocalypse"—Sediq was second in command to their supreme leader, Hibatullah Akhundzada, hiding under guard, somewhere in Pakistan. Qayoumi held the power of life or death over his men, and issuing reminders of that fact never got old.

"Sir, I will have to calculate that number for you more precisely. I can go now, if you wish, and—"

"Never mind." Sediq waved that suggestion off as if it were a gnat buzzing around his head. "What have we learned, if anything, from the Crusader who was slain?"

"A white man, as you know, sir. He carried no papers or other identifying articles. No military dog tags, no—"

"I understand the term, Ehsan."

"Of course, sir. His clothing was unremarkable, no labels, tags or other markings that would trace it to a source. The weapons, likewise, may be found in every corner of the world, serial numbers thoroughly removed. He has two scars, one likely from an appendectomy, the other from an old leg injury below the left knee, both long healed. He has no *alqulfa*, but in the West today that does not make him Jewish."

"I don't care if he's circumcised, Ehsan. That tells me less than nothing."

"No, sir. As you say."

"What do we know about the one who got away?"

"Armed with a 5.45mm weapon, doubtless a Kalashnikov, likely AKS-74U like the dead Crusader's gun. One short, efficient burst eliminated Sandjar Kahn, and his killer escaped before the other sentries could react."

"Before they could react?" Sediq made no attempt to mask his mockery. "Were they asleep, perhaps?"

"No, sir."

"Nor playing cards, perhaps? *Panjar* or *dosdakaan?*"

"No, sir. I promise you."

"Still, an example should be made."

"I understand, sir. If you have someone in mind..."

"The choice is yours, Ehsan. How many other sentries were there?"

"Besides Sandjar, five."

"Pick one at random. Have the others watch. Do it yourself."

Another flush ascending from the collar of Ehsan Abarkhyl's khaki shirt. "It shall be done, sir," he replied.

"Without delay."

"As you command, sir."

"Yes. *Kama 'umirt.* As I command."

"If there is nothing else, sir..."

"There is still one infidel at large, Ehsan."

"Yes, of course."

"My preference would be to capture him alive, for questioning."

"If possible. I understand, sir."

"Even if he proves resistant to interrogation, he may still be useful."

"An exchange, sir?"

"By no means. For a future broadcast."

"Ah."

Thus far, ISIL—the Islamic State of Iraq and the Levant—had posted videotaped beheadings of various foreign hostages worldwide on social media, at least nineteen decapitations carried out by chief executioner Mohammed Emwazi, dubbed "Jihadi John" by certain infidel reporters. Two American drones supposedly killed Emwazi at Raqqa, Syria in November 2015, though rumors of his survival persisted, and alternate "Jihadi Johns" had been identified as a West London rapper and a Portsmouth computer hacker.

When all else failed, jihadists could at least keep the Crusaders guessing, looking over their shoulders for lethal shadows.

"And if he won't be taken, sir?"

"Hard proof that he is done. His head and *alkhisiatayn*, Ehsan. Not on a silver platter, mind you. Any plate will do."

Abarkhyl plainly did not know if he should laugh or not. Instead, he nodded, risked a narrow smile, and said, "Exactly as you wish, sir."

"Be off about your business then. And Ehsan?"

"Yes, sir?"

"Do not fail."

Caracas

Simón Bolívar International is the largest of Venezuela's sixty-seven public airports, boasting two asphalt runways measuring 9,930 and 11,483 feet. Once an aviation gateway to South America, moving an average five million passengers yearly, it has fallen on hard times since 2014, losing twenty-three international carriers by March 2019, while only twenty remain, plus seven regional cargo carriers. Annual passenger traffic has slumped to an average 560,000.

Multiple crises beset the nation's flagship airport, most traceable to President Maduro's corrupt and inefficient government. Terminals commonly lack air-conditioning, even electricity and running water. The airport's chief sanitation handler went bankrupt, producing frequently deplorable conditions. Some airlines divert their flights from fear of Simón Bolívar's endemic crime. Bolivarian National Guardsmen, tasked with providing airport security, often extort tourists at gunpoint.

In December 2018 the Russian Air Force deployed two Tupolev Tu-160 bombers "for exercises" at the airport, in a clear show of force. Three months later, two more military planes arrived, bearing one hundred soldiers and thirty-five tons of hardware. The message was obvious, even to *El Presidente* and his cabinet: hands off Aeroflot passengers, at least, or there'd be hell to pay.

Today, the airport's management was nursing cautious hope. They'd planned some overdue expansion, constructing new international gates and clearing part of an old parking lot to put up an airport hotel. Whether they would succeed without a change in the political regime was anybody's guess, but Nicolás Maduro showed no signs of loosening his stranglehold on Venezuela anytime in the near future.

Cody had no fear of passing through the airport on his own. He'd left his weapons in the semi rig, abandoned on an access road adjacent to the long-term parking lot, and hoofed it in with nothing but his carryon. If any Guardsmen hassled him, he'd slip them a few Bolívars in lieu of crippling them and bringing down more heat. As for the rest, booking a flight and killing time until he took off for the first leg of his journey halfway round the globe, it all came down to hurry up and wait.

He sought to travel from Caracas to Kabul, specifically to Hamid Karzai International Airport. To start that trek, Jack chose Iberia, the Spanish airline, flying out of Simón Bolívar to Adolfo Suárez Madrid–Barajas Airport after a layover at Humberto Delgado Airport in Lisbon. From Madrid he hoped to pick up Middle East Airlines and land at Beirut–Rafic Hariri International. It would be dicey after that—commercial options ran toward Royal Jordanian, Saudi, Royal Maroc—or he could go in hock and try a private charter, maybe even off the books.

Whatever.

With his one-way ticket on Iberia in hand, Cody was virtually on his way. Now all he had to do was kill four hours till his flight was called, assuming that it left on time. His stomach growled, but Jack wasn't inclined to trust the airport's restaurants, so he stopped into a convenience shop and loaded up on junk food: brands he recognized by name, within their sell-by dates, adding two mini-cans of Pepsi and snagging a

Greg Iles paperback he hadn't read.

Lugging his purchases in a recyclable paper bag, he walked to the Iberia departure gate and found a corner seat that let him scan the concourse with a solid wall behind him while he snacked and started reading *Mississippi Blood*.

Two guys in military uniforms passed by, wearing maroon berets that marked them as National Guardsmen, rather than regular troops whose were black. Both carried standard-issue AK-103 assault rifles and tried to strut but lacked the basic military bearing. One of them eyed Cody in his plastic chair but they moved on without stopping to ask for cash.

Only the lower ranks were common thieves, although corruption permeated to the very top, as with the other agencies in President Maduro's little world. Not long ago, the stateside DEA had blown the cover on a Venezuelan cocaine-smuggling ring that called itself the Cartel of the Suns. The "suns" in question were gold insignia worn on the uniforms of certain generals—both regular army and National Guard— who ran the network for Maduro and his family. None were indicted or jailed, but the U.S. Treasury Department's Office of Foreign Assets Control had sanctioned officials including the nation's Vice President, Army Intelligence chief, and two consecutive Guard commanders.

No wonder that Maduro raged nonstop about "imperialists" meddling in his country's national affairs, when most of said affairs were crimes.

When the Guardsmen had moved on, Jack turned back to his book but couldn't focus on the story, busy thinking about

Sara stranded somewhere in Afghanistan. He wondered whether she was even still alive, and if not, what she might have suffered before coming to her private end of days.

Forcing his mind away from those stark images, Cody decided that in any case, his solitary course of action would remain unchanged. If Sara was alive, his top priority was finding and removing her from a virtually lawless nation that amounted to a nightmare parody of the American Wild West.

If she was dead…

There'd obviously be no rescue in that case, but there *would* be revenge. Whoever played a part in Sara's fare would be on Cody's list, names presently unknown, and he'd devote himself to hounding them relentlessly, from whatever positions they might occupy, until he'd seen them all consigned to early graves.

And if that vengeance cost his life, so what?

Cody had spent each moment of his so-called life, since the annihilation of his family, chasing oblivion across a blighted battleground.

Afghanistan, he thought, would be as good a place to run it down and face the bitter end as anywhere on Earth.

The White House

No one other than a love-struck aide or intern got excited by a presidential summons. Moving through the West Wing of the White House toward the Oval Office, Denham Boyd flashed back to images of schoolboy days and being called upon to face the principal. Those trips had been traumatic in his youth, and this was worse.

The Top Man almost never called for anyone to share good news.

Jessica Stone, the president's pet dragon, met Boyd with a look that seemed to say, "*What took you so damned long?*" She didn't even try to fake a smile as she got on the intercom, saying, "It's Mister Boyd to see you, sir."

The too-familiar voice came back, reduced in volume, with a tinny echo. "Send him in."

"He'll see you know," Jessica said, unnecessarily.

Boyd circled wide around her desk and stepped into the Oval Office, pausing for a beat to wonder—as he always did—whether he ought to knock regardless of the secretary's terse instruction. Even as the thought took shape, Boyd knew it was ridiculous, but he still closed the door softly behind him once he was inside.

He almost said, "You rang?" but caught himself at the last second, settling for, "How may I help you, Mister President?"

The Man was on his feet behind the same desk used by predecessors dating back to Franklin Roosevelt, a gift from Britain's Queen Victoria, made out of timbers from the British frigate HMS *Resolute*, trapped in Arctic ice in 1854, recovered by a crew of U.S. seamen. He was flanked by flags—Old Glory and the Presidential Seal, also appearing on the office carpet—beyond which three tall southward-facing windows overlooked the White House grounds.

The Oval Office has four doors: to the northeast, the one through which Denham had entered; on the west, for access to a private dining room and study; to the west, an exit onto the Rose Garden; and on the northwest, serving the West Wing.

None offered Denham Boyd a getaway.

"Help me?" The Man frowned while considering his words. "I hope you can, Denham."

"Yes, sir?"

"Tell me about Afghanistan."

Coming from someone else, that might have been a general request for information: history and politics, America's ongoing war that had no end in sight, drug-trafficking, even the climate. In this case, however, Boyd knew it could only mean one thing.

"There's still no word, sir."

"That's your answer, is it? 'Still no word'?"

"Sir—"

"Do you know why I keep you around, Boyd?"

"As a personal advisor, sir."

"Correct. So, if it's not too inconvenient, earn your paycheck, son. *Advise* me as to why there's 'still no word.' Can you do that?"

"Sir—"

Interrupting him, The Man pressed on. "Because when I hear 'still no word,' it makes me think someone's been sleeping on the job."

"I can assure you, Mister President, that's not the case."

"And yet, you say—"

It was Boyd's turn to interrupt. "Sir, Seal Team X is gearing up and getting ready for insertion as we speak."

"And there's another phrase that makes me wonder. 'Getting ready'."

"Sir?"

"The Joint Chiefs tell me we've got special teams in readiness around the clock. If something breaks, they're on it. Are my Joint Chiefs lying to me, Boyd?"

"No, sir. But there are transportation issues, as I'm sure you understand. We have seven Naval Special Warfare Group, consisting of fourteen SEAL teams, sir. All seven groups have stateside headquarters, in California and Virginia."

"I don't need a travelogue. Cut to the chase."

"Yes, sir. Unless deployed for action in a given theater of war, SEAL teams—while constantly in readiness—must be transported to an area of operation as required."

"And we have no one in Afghanistan? After how many years of fighting there?"

"Sixteen, sir. We have troops in place, of course, but not a SEAL team standing by. No Delta Force contingent, and no Air Force Special Tactics Squadrons. SEAL Team X is airborne now, sir, but the distance from Virginia to Kabul is seven thousand miles. Say fifteen hours' transit time."

"Arriving when?" the president inquired.

Boyd had to check his watch on that, before he said, "Six hours until touchdown, give or take, sir. Then they airlift to coordinates provided by our asset in the field."

"And then we'll see some action?"

"One way or another. Yes, sir."

"You need work on your delivery," The Man advised. "The way you lay things out, I don't suggest you set your sights on politics. The voters need encouragement, not 'one way or another,' yada-yada."

"No, sir. Thank you, sir."

"For what?"

"Your good advice."

The president considered that, frowning, then turned away to face the tall windows behind him. "Six hours, plus some time to locate those coordinates," he said. "Let's call it seven hours. I'll expect some information then. Dismissed."

Boyd nearly thanked the president but caught himself in time, turned on his heel and left the Oval Office, heading for his own.

Seven hours.

It didn't sound like much, from one perspective, but for people on the ground, hunting or being hunted in Afghanistan, it might turn out to be a lifetime.

One way or another, right.

CHAPTER 3

Baghlan Province, Afghanistan

Sara Durell was making decent time, considering that she could only travel after nightfall, with no access to a motor vehicle of any kind, while she was being hunted by the Taliban.

So far she'd put Bamyan Province behind her without being spotted, either by the jihadists intent on killing her or by what passed for native law enforcement—meaning both the Afghan National Police and Afghan Local Police, both underpaid and often under fire, chiefly engaged in busting farmers who "forgot" to pay the mandatory tax on cultivating opium.

Other stumbling blocks included the Afghan Public Protection Force, subordinate to the Islamic Republic's Ministry of the Interior, created in theory to protect specific people, infrastructure, facilities and construction projects. In short, glorified rent-a-cops assigned chiefly to foreign corporations operating in the war-torn country—which, in most cases, also employed private military companies based in the U.S. or Western Europe.

The cherry on top of that sundae was the Afghan National Army, supplemented by units of the NATO-led International-al Security Assistance Force. Both spent most of their time stalking Taliban insurgents and, incidentally, any fugitives on the run who said Taliban might seek to capture or kill.

In short: there was lots of law and very little order in Afghanistan, which helped to cover Sara's tracks on the one hand, and made her life doubly dangerous on the other.

Baghlan Province, Bamyan's neighbor to the northeast, was larger than Bamyan, at 8,154 square miles and an esti-mated 910,000 population versus 5,473 square miles and some 425,000 inhabitants. Its terrain was much the same—rocky and mountainous, with open desert stretches in between the ranges—but it had no Afghan Local Police, making do with the ANP Afghan National Security Forces assisted by NATO.

Essentially, that meant more hiding, traveling afoot by night, avoiding anyone who posed a risk—and that meant everyone. Deprived of her interpreter, Sara couldn't commu-nicate aside from crude sign language or the weapons she was carrying, and if she played that card, someone would likely have to die.

Her goal, traveling northward, might be either Kunduz Province or Takhar Province, both butting up against the border of Uzbekistan and safety of a sort, if she could make it that far on her own. Associated problems on that grueling journey, leaving out the gunmen hunting her with murderous intent, were food, water, and any risks tossed up at her by the Afghan terrain.

Food-wise, Sara was getting by on MREs—Meals, Ready-to-Eat in backwards U.S. military-speak—which just might see her through one meal daily on her trek. The eight-by-four-inch plastic bags, date coded, offered a dozen different entrees plus crackers, fruit-flavored candies, raisins, a fig bar, instant coffee, seasonings, plastic utensils, a flameless heater, napkins and toilet paper.

Soldiers in a combat zone normally consumed three MREs per day, but Sara was traveling light, on short rations. Call it the run-for-your-life freaking diet. Granted, she had been bikini-ready on arrival in Afghanistan. The challenge now was getting through it without looking like a frail escapee from a concentration camp.

Or hell, just getting out alive.

One point in her favor, barely, was a Raveon model M7 GX, doubling as a GPS transponder for tracking and a radio modem for sending or receiving data. If her luck held out and help was on the way—a huge "if" in her present circumstances—Sara could be spotted via satellite, a rescue orchestrated and achieved.

If not…

Then she was absolutely on her own, with a good chance of being killed.

If that turned out to be the case, she didn't plan on going down alone.

Adolfo Suárez Madrid–Barajas Airport, Spain

Madrid's pitstop was a vast improvement over Caracas. Europe's second-largest airport after Paris–Charles de Gaulle, at 7,500 acres, it featured four runways and five passenger terminals. In terms of traffic, it ranked as Europe's sixth busiest, moving fifty-eight million passengers last year.

That was perfect for Jack Cody, a crowded complex to get lost in, hoping no one from the White House or the CIA had spooks out looking for him yet. His passport was "legitimate"—meaning only his name and other information had been falsified, using a blank passport issued by Great Britain's General Register Office. It had passed inspection in Caracas and should serve him here as well, before he swapped it out to make the next leg of his journey eastward.

Jack was dining in one of the restaurants available in Terminal T3, enjoying Spanish food—or as the natives called it, simply "food"—including seafood *paella* and *ropa vieja*, washed down with Mahou Classica beer. He had acquired a one-way ticket to Beirut as planned, flying with Middle East Airlines, but still had ample time to kill before departure.

And no matter how he dawdled, Cody couldn't seem to get away from time.

He was intensely conscious of its passage, constantly reminded by his Grand Seiko 9F quartz movement wristwatch and various wall-mounted clocks throughout the airport. Kabul was two and a half hours ahead of him right now, but getting there would take a good deal longer, followed up by preparations on the ground.

All that, before he even started homing in on Sara.

Too much time to kill, in every sense.

He'd reached out from mid-air, between Caracas and Lisbon, touching base with a techie friend at the CIA's George Bush Center for Intelligence in Langley, Virginia. The friend had provided details on Sara's GPS transponder and left the door open for check-ins while Jack was in transit, giving him up-to-the-minute locations for contact, but there were still two problems.

First, locating the transponder didn't mean that he would find Sara Durell still packing it around.

Second, he might go through the motions, tracking down both Sara and the GPS device, only to find that she was dead.

If that turned out to be the case, how would he then proceed? Like freaking hell on wheels.

If Sara was beyond his earthly help, Jack might not know immediately who had put her down. But someone *always* knows, and Cody would start rattling cages, keeping it up until something shook loose and fell into his hands. Whatever was required to find the individuals responsible, he'd get it done—and then, when he was certain of his targets, retribution would commence.

And no one in the neighborhood would ever be the same again.

If any neighborhood remained standing.

Northeast Afghanistan

"Five minutes," Master Chief Petty Officer Ben Austin informed the other members of his eight-man unit, code-named SEAL Team X. As their advanced special operations commander, whatever happened now, from this point onward, would be his responsibility.

The buck stopped here.

The other members of his team, in descending order of rank, included two Second Chief Petty Officers, Leroy Byers and Carl Shugari; Chief Petty Officer Dakota Webster; Petty Officer First Class Kyle Swenson; Petty Officer Second Class Travis Monsoor; and two Petty Officers Third Class, Arnold Petri and Harry Takazi.

While trained in all tactics from jump school to underwater demolition, each member of Seal Team X also had his specialty honed to a fine razor's edge. Byers, their only African American, was the sniper. Shugari handled technical surveillance and explosive ordinance disposal. Webster was their navigator, including functions as lead driver and point man. Swenson was Webster's backup navigator, well versed in rural and urban protective security. Monsoor did double duty as their breacher and interrogator. Petri was their communicator and corpsman. Takazi—a Yonsei descendant of Japanese immigrants—was lead climber and handled sensitive site exploration.

Gear-wise, six members of the crew carried M4A1 carbines with semi-automatic and fully automatic firing modes, chambered in 5.56×45mm NATO, three of the six with under-barrel M203 40mm grenade launchers attached. All eight wore HK45CT pistols—the Heckler & Koch Compact Technical model chambered for .45 ACP and carried MK 3 Navy Knives with black handles and clip-point blades.

The odd men out for long guns were Byers, packing an M82 Barrett .50-caliber extreme long-range anti-material rifle for sniping, and Monsoor, armed with an M4 Benelli Super 90 shotgun. The semi-automatic twelve-gauge handled any shells ranging from birdshot to sabot slugs, plus specialty numbers including breaching rounds, gas-filled ferret rounds, piranha rounds full of sharp tacks, and dragon's breath incendiary rounds.

Something for everyone.

The M203 launchers, likewise, fed a range of 40mm rounds including high explosive M386 grenades, M397A1 air burst rounds, and MP-APERS canisters, each loaded with twenty metal pellets weighing a half-ounce a piece.

In terms of hand-lobbed ordnance, each member of the team was dressed to kill with M61 antipersonnel fragmentation grenades, M14 incendiary bombs, M15 "willie peters" to spew white phosphorus smoke, and Model 308-1 napalm grenades designed specifically with U.S. Navy SEALs in mind.

On top of that, they carried blocks of CR plastic explosive for making strategic shaped charges, with timed detonators set for a range from five minutes to three full hours. If there was a battlefield contingency omitted from their plan, MCPO

Austin had no idea what it might be.

An eight-man team could face much larger hostile forces and emerge victorious, but MCPO Austin knew that any battle could go either way, depending on a wide variety of factors that included weather and geography, the personal commitment of fanatical opponents, or something simpler, like a slipup that surrendered the advantage of surprise.

Their current rescue mission didn't please Austin—risking his team to pull one wayward spook out of the frying pan—but he was under orders, and the gung-ho MCPO *always* followed orders. As Alfred, Lord Tennyson said in his most famous poem, years before the U.S. Civil War, "Theirs not to reason why, theirs but to do and die."

The flight's jump master called time, and MCPO Austin led the way, trailed by his seven men, each weighted with a primary and backup parachute in addition to their other gear. Today the plan was for a HAHO jump—*h*igh *a*ltitude, *h*igh *o*pening—the opposite of HALO, which was free-falling from high altitude and opening your chute much closer to the ground. HAHO jumping was more difficult, more dangerous, and required hours of extra training to open chutes in tandem, seconds after exiting the plane, and form a "stack" to stay together, keeping the SEALs in a tight group for landing.

The trick could either let you safely enter hostile territory, or result in getting every jumper killed, depending on what lay below.

The SEALs attached their static lines and quick-stepped toward the aircraft's open bay. Then the rush of wind was strong in Austin's face and he was plummeting, counting the seconds till his canopy snapped open and arrested his descent with all the delicacy of a head-on auto crash.

And this would be another crucial danger point, before they even set foot on the rocky ground below.

Unknown to most Americans, Navy SEALs and other secretive military units had suffered eleven parachute-related deaths between 2011 and 2015—a 60 percent increase over the prior five-year period—but only one had made headlines so far, the loss of SEAL Commander Jason Kortz during 2015's Fleet Week exercises off the coast of Southern California. The Pentagon had ruled that case "preventable" and blamed some training officers, but answers in the other deaths were still being investigated, likely to be kept forever under wraps.

And on a job like this, over Afghanistan, MCPO Austin knew that no stateside newsies would be privy to whatever happened next.

Feeling the other members of his team stack up behind him and above, he wondered if he should have gone to chapel before flying out, but then he focused on his mission and the spy they'd come to rescue, knowing he could only do his best.

And that was pretty goddamned good.

DATELINE
Bamyan Province

"And still no sign of the escapee?"

Sediq Qayoumi did not care for Mohammed Ali Isani's tone or attitude, a condescension both infuriating and misplaced. Although he wore no uniform or rank insignia, Isani was a captain with Pakistan's Inter-Services Intelligence, specifically the ISI's Covert Action Division, responsible for paramilitary operations and other "special" tasks on par with those performed by the CIA's Special Activities Division.

Isani's current job was serving as liaison between leaders of the Taliban and ISI's headquarters along Khayaban-e-Suharwardy, in Islamabad's Aabpara Market. He was arrogant and supercilious, a constant irritant in Qayoumi's life, but there was nothing to be done about it. In these years, nearly two decades since the Crusader invasion of 2001, the ISI provided much of the financial and material support for Taliban activities.

The rest, of course, derived from heroin and human trafficking in Allah's name.

"No contact yet," Qayoumi granted, grudgingly. "The search continues."

"But for how much longer, may I ask? How long before the enemy escapes entirely and exposes all out secrets to the West at large?"

Qayoumi took a breath and held it for a micro-second, just to calm himself. "That will not happen," he assured Captain Isani. "When we overtake the man we seek—"

"The man?" Isani interrupted him. "Are you quite sure of that, Sediq?"

Qayoumi blinked at his unwelcome visitor. "What do you mean?"

"My people, after analyzing boot prints from the murder scene—those not destroyed by your over-excited soldiers—tell me they are smaller than the normal prints left by a man shod in equivalent footwear."

"What are you saying? That a *child* killed one of my sentries and managed to elude the rest?"

"No, not a child," Isani answered, toying with Qayoumi. "But, just possibly, a woman."

"That's ridiculous," Qayoumi answered back, but niggling doubt had already set in. "Crusaders would not send a female on a mission of this sort, surely."

"Why not?" Isani challenged him. Before Qayoumi could respond, the captain forged ahead. "Are you aware that sixteen percent of all U.S. military troops deployed worldwide, and eighteen percent of their officer corps, are women? Six years ago, their Pentagon announced admission of females into their most elite fighting units—the Navy SEALs, Army Rangers and Special Forces, take your pick."

"I pick none of them," Qayoumi said. "Women are not and never will be suitable for combat, much less in a role of leadership."

"So *you* say. But a woman—Gina Haspel; look her up, Sediq—is presently director of their CIA. One of eight agents killed in the 1983 Beirut embassy bombing was a woman, Monique Lewis."

Qayoumi snorted. Muttered, "Probably a secretary."

"Not at all. You are behind the times, Sediq. I fear you won't learn current events from poring over the Quran."

"You verge on blasphemy, Mohammed."

"Yet, I have the Prophet's name—and I am sanctioned by the strictest Muslim government on Earth."

"Is there a point to this?" Qayoumi asked.

"Just this: your bias blinds you to one half of the world's population, Sediq. In this special case, it may have set you on the wrong path in pursuit of our elusive enemy and given *her* sufficient lead time to escape."

"I don't believe it."

"You remind me of the die-hard skeptic who abandons logic. A true skeptic keeps an open mind. He says, 'I will believe it when I see it.' But knee-jerk deniers answer that by saying, 'We'll *see* it when we *believe* it.' Can you work out the distinction?"

"I'm not an idiot, Captain."

"I hope not," said Isani, not quite sneering. "While you cogitate on what I've said, my men are broadening their search, including women in the profile and detaining any who appear suspicious."

"That invites police to interfere, perhaps the army, even NATO."

"Have they not been interfering in your country for the better part of twenty years, Sediq? Your efforts to resist, much less expel them, have been disappointing to observers near and far."

"Including you, no doubt."

"I take my orders from Director-General Asim Munir, as he takes his from Prime Minister Imran Khan and Minister of Defense Pervez Khattak. You, on the other hand, rely on me for your material support, except when you are smuggling poison to heroin addicts in violation of the Quran."

"How dare you?"

"Easily," Isani answered. "After brief investigation of our mutual problem, I have already found a major defect in your effort to resolve it. That must be corrected...or, regrettably, I must find someone else who's more amendable to reason."

Qayoumi recognized the threat, not even thinly veiled, and stopped himself from answering in anger. Rather, he politely tipped his head and told the Pakistani, "I completely understand, Captain. To hear is to obey."

Beirut–Rafic Hariri International Airport

Beirut and its airport had shared a tragic history for over half a century, since 1968. Most of the wounds were self-inflicted, with substantial "help" from Israel, but Jack Cody never passed through Lebanon without considering what might have been without religion's meddling in the realm of politics.

Jack knew the trouble had begun with French rule, with a parliamentary system that favored Maronite Christians over the country's Shia and Sunni Muslims. Nazis threw the French out during World War Two, then Britain gave a nod to "God's word" five years later, by creating Israel and uprooting many of its previous Muslim inhabitants. A hundred thousand of those refugees fled into Lebanon and started plotting to recapture Palestine from Jews they viewed as hostile usurpers.

So passed Phase One.

In 1968 some Palestinians attacked an El Al flight in Athens, prompting Israel to assault Beirut's airport, effectively destroying two-thirds of Lebanon's aviation industry, leaving Middle East Airlines as the country's only carrier. Beirut International—soon renamed—lost its status as the Mideast's premier travel hub, but there was worse to come.

In April 1975 Lebanon embarked on a fifteen-year civil war, fanatical Christians and Muslims seeking mutual destruction, killing an estimated 120,000 persons in the names of their respective deities. Another million Lebanese took off for other countries, and even today, some 76,000 remained displaced inside the country of their birth. Airport renovation began in 1977, largely undone when Israelis shelled Beirut–Rafic Hariri five years later. In 1982 jihadists bombed a U.S. military barracks, killing 241 servicemen, then rebounded in '83 with an embassy blast that killed another seventeen Americans, plus forty-six Lebanese nationals.

Outside peacekeeping forces finally restored a semblance of order in 1990, though sporadic mayhem continued. Airport reconstruction moved ahead, with runway overhauls and construction of a new terminal that took twelve years to finish, handling six million passengers yearly and shooting for sixteen million by 2035, if no one went crazy and lit another doomsday fuse.

Today Beirut–Rafic Hariri was Lebanon's only commercial airport, serving a country of six million people, welcoming some two million tourists yearly. Since few sane people vacation in impoverished "former" war zones, most of those visitors were rapacious business types, providing ten percent of Lebanon's annual GNP while grasping for anything they could take home, chiefly historical antiquities and heroin, processed by warlords in the still-lawless Beqaa Valley. The government, such as it was, placed no restrictions on influx of foreign capital, which made Lebanon an oligarch's play-ground.

Located six miles from downtown Beirut, in the capital's southern suburbs, Beirut–Rafic Hariri International is home to many literal fly-by-night charter airlines, created this week, bankrupt the next, reborn with a new name the week after that. Nobody cared, as long as ample bribes kept flowing to authorities and there were no embarrassments such as drug busts or murders on the tarmac.

Bottom line, it fit Jack Cody's needs to the proverbial tee.

Now all he had to do was find a charter company that fit his needs—no questions asked—and wouldn't try to rip him off, forcing Cody to kill them all and steal a plane himself.

Simple. Like stepping accidentally into an open grave.

CHAPTER 4

Baghlan Province

Sara's Raveon transponder told her help was on the way and gave her GPS coordinates for the meet-up. Checking the box now, she saw that she'd made it to 35.8043° North, 69.2878° East with a quarter-hour to spare.

Now it came down to that old classic order from the military: Hurry up and wait.

There were a ton of things that the M7 GX couldn't tell her, starting at the top with how many fanatical hostiles were hunting her right now and where they were. She couldn't hear the hue and cry, which meant one of two things: either her trackers hadn't zeroed on her trail yet, or they might be close enough to play it stealthy, creeping up to bring her within range and take her down.

Sara Durell had done her best to minimize the traces that she'd left behind, from inadvertent contact with the enemy to where she huddled in the gray of falling dusk right now, not quite a full day since she'd seen her partner die, and capped his killer in return.

She'd changed direction time and time again, staying on rocky ground whenever possible to leave no visible footprints, and dragging hacked-off limbs of Pashtun juniper behind her over sandy soil to wipe away her tracks.

She'd made good use of streams whenever she encountered them, knowing they likely had no tracking dogs, but erring on the side of caution, and had skirted wide around the rural homes she passed, except for when she'd stopped at one to supplement her dwindling store of water.

Her one meal for the day has been MRE Menu 6: a beef taco with "Santa Fe style" rice and beans, tortillas and cheddar cheese spread, a nut and fruit mix with M&Ms, and a sugar-free, orange-flavored beverage base. "Accessory Packet B" contained instant coffee and dry creamer, a tea bag, sugar, chewing gum, a paper towel and napkin, with a "stimulator, interdental" that turned out to be a plastic toothpick.

No one complicated simple English quite like the armed forces, where a ballpoint pen became a "reproducing medium," torture was "enhanced interrogation," and "pockets" was applied to shrink serious problems, as when swarms of *fedayeen* became "pockets of resistance" or hordes of starving civilians converted to "pockets of need".

All bullshit, all the time—but she had learned to play the game and live with it, as long as her actions engendered positive results.

A quick glance at her watch told Sara that ten minutes still remained before projected contact with her rescuers. Beyond knowing they'd be Americans, she couldn't guess which military unit had been called upon to lift her out, or how precisely they intended to achieve that goal. There were at least ten Special Operations Units spread across three branches of the U.S. military—Army, Navy and Air Force—but who had been selected for this rescue mission would depend on placement when the call went out, allowing for the shortest ETA.

Eight minutes now, and Sara didn't care who came to fetch her, just as long as they came heavy, with a lift-off plan that worked. She understood the mission's built-in limitations, time and distance, balancing the team's optimal size and armament against potential hostile odds. Its members wouldn't know who they were coming to extract or why, only that it was top priority with no margin for error.

It was do-or-die time, and a single fact was foremost on her mind.

If the warfighters sent to extricate her died, most likely so would she.

And if she lived, imprisoned by the Taliban or Pakistani ISI, that would be even worse.

In that case, she'd be grilled until she broke or found a way to kill herself. And even if she *did* break, spilled her guts on camera for all the world to see, the only exit waiting for her from captivity would be another video in which she played the role of human sacrifice.

Which was exactly why Sara had steeled herself to save

one bullet, if and when the final firefight came.

And use it on herself.

Hamid Karzai International Airport, Kabul

Afghanistan's premier airport doubles as one of its largest military bases. Since the American invasion of 2001, Hamid Karzai International—three miles from the capital's center—has sprouted facilities serving the U.S. Air Force, Afghan Air Force, and NATO's International Security Assistance Force, more than one hundred warplanes overall.

The airport has also expanded civilian facilities over the past decade, including a new international terminal, relegating the older Soviet-built original to domestic flights only. Its single runway, measuring 11,500 feet, serves ten passenger airlines and seven cargo carriers, but hangars are reserved for military planes, as are the airport's seven helipads. These days, the greatest volume of commercial traffic—four separate airlines with multiple flights per day—transport travelers back and forth from Dubai International Airport, 1,048 miles southwest of Kabul, in the United Arab Emirates.

A pair of staffers from the U.S. Embassy on Massoud Circle met Jack Cody on arrival, with the gear he had requested and sufficient information for him to proceed. His transport from Hamid Karzai into the field would be a UH-60 Black Hawk helicopter operated by the CIA, the gear he had requested in advance already stowed on board.

Inspecting it while he absorbed details of his impending jaunt, Cody checked off the items from his wish list. The assault rifle was a Russian AK-107, chambered in 5.45×39mm, with a GP-25 *Kostyor* ("Bonfire") 40mm grenade launcher mounted under its barrel. Bandoleers held the spare magazines and an assortment of grenades to feed the launcher if he needed them.

Jack's sidearm was a Glock 21, each magazine containing thirteen .45-caliber ACP rounds. A dozen Russian F1 frag grenades were also clipped onto his combat webbing. If the shit went hand-to-hand, he'd be relying on a KA-BAR USMC fighting knife with a seven-inch anodized blade.

The outfit waiting for him on the Black Hawk included United Shield Spec Ops Delta Mid Cut X-harness Ballistic Helmet; a Desert Camouflage Uniform mottled with a three-color pattern of beige, dark brown and pale green; with a pair of temperate and hot weather mountain combat boots. Aside from ammo bandoleers, he would be slipping on an olive-green Mil-Tech USMC tactical vest and a MOLLE pack—pronounced "Molly", short for modular lightweight load-carrying equipment—that included a hydration bladder, obviating requirement of a separate canteen.

While Jack was getting dressed and strapping on his gear, the older member of his welcoming committee—"Ross", if you could trust him—ran down details of the operation as it stood. A SEAL team was en route to rendezvous with Sara, hopefully extracting her without hang-ups, but Jack had memorized one simple rule of thumb: "No plan survives first contact with the enemy."

Jack hoped the SEALs could pull it off and spare him humping through the boonies trying to catch up with Sara, but he wasn't counting on it.

No one bothered introducing Cody to the Black Hawk's two-man crew, men younger than himself, both sporting cultivated facial hair. Why should he get to know them anyway? They had a job to do, as Cody did, and would have been instructed to forget him once they'd dropped him off, no sitrep filed in writing for the Company.

The sooner they unloaded him, the better it would be for all concerned.

The choppers twin General Electric T700-GE-701C turboshaft engines revved on the tarmac, fifty-four-foot rotors gaining speed above the Black Hawk's fuselage before they lifted off. Below them, as they rose, the guy whose parents might have named him Ross waved once, then turned away to join his partner in their armored Toyota Land Cruiser.

Jack watched them from the Black Hawk's open bay until they faded out of sight, then turned his face toward war.

Baghlan Province

MCPO Ben Austin stopped short at a silent signal from their point man, CPO Dakota Webster. Up ahead, he saw Webster consulting his transponder and confirming that they'd nearly reached the GPS coordinates where they should find the spook they had been ordered to extract if possible, or to eliminate if not.

Austin took time to check his own transponder and confirm the information. They were presently within a thousand yards of 35.8043° North, 69.2878° East. As to what actually waited for them there...well, they would simply have to wait and see.

Their contact might be waiting for them, anxious to depart, possibly wounded, maybe even dead. Worst case scenario, if they arrived to find the spook already captured by the Taliban and ISI advisers, there was bound to be a fight. Same thing if Afghan regulars had stumbled on the scene and made the bust.

Their mission had been ranked Top Secret/Critical, meaning that no natives on either side of the eighteen-year insurgency could be allowed to find out what was going on. That was the reason Austin and his men were in the dark regarding details, even a description of their contact on the ground withheld from them.

Master Chief Austin disliked going into battle with a set of blinders on, but it was nothing new to him. By definition Navy SEALs were handed covert missions, hit and run, with no details beyond what their superiors believed might prove essential to success. They lived, fought, died by certain basic rules: adhere to orders, leave no member of the team behind, but when the shooting started, no one could foretell what happened next.

Having a sure-fire psychic on the team would have enhanced their capabilities, but Austin had no faith in all that witchy shit. He only knew what he could see through gunsights or be satellite telemetry, but mostly he trusted what lay in front of him, within his reach.

Whatever he could see, hear, touch or kill.

Out front, Dakota Webster dropped his upraised fist and started moving forward, taking each step individually now, as if he was advancing through a mine field. MCPO Austin followed cautiously, the other members of his team strung out behind him, close enough to help if shooting started, but not clumped together as an easy target for their enemies.

And in Afghanistan, as in so many other places they had served, the enemy was everywhere. Men, women, even children could surprise you with a hideout gun or an explosive vest and take you down before you had a fix on what was happening.

Unless you saw it coming first and took the necessary action.

Do it unto others, before they did it to you.

A thousand yards isn't that far in broad daylight—less than four football fields, a clear shot with the proper scope and rifle—but at night, on unfamiliar ground, it sometimes feels like miles. Austin wished that they had a Predator on station overhead, spotting for hostiles in hiding, but that had been ruled out by headquarters as "too intrusive" for their covert op.

So, SEAL Team X was on its own, for good or ill. They were prepared to cope with anything in theory, but battlefield

experience had taught the MCPO that a yawning void sometimes lay in between theory and practice.

Sometimes, if you didn't watch your step, that could turn
out to be the mouth of Hell.

Omar Jamalzadah paused and listened to the night. Somewhere off to the east, a nightjar gave its rattling call, sounding
like worn machinery in need of oil. A dormouse squealed in
panic as an owl swooped down upon it, talons poised. Wing-
less bush crickets, some up to four inches long, sang from the
shrubbery, calling for mates or—in the case of one voracious
predatory species—living prey.

A bit like me, thought Jamalzadah, *though I do not sing*.

And he was a *talibé*—"student"—from which the name
Taliban was derived. American Crusaders, in their ignorance,
referred to individual guerrillas of the Taliban themselves
as "Talibans", although the term was plural as it stood and
tacking on an "s" was meaningless. That was the very least
of Yankee sins in Omar's estimation, but he sometimes seized
upon it as a token of what made him hate the Western infidels
so much.

His team of twenty men were on the hunt for an unknown
intruder, one of two who'd run afoul of his superiors the night
before this, killing one defender of the faith and losing one of
their own people in return. At first Jamalzadah's instructions
specified a male target, no known description, but the order
had been recently updated to suggest their prey might actually

be a woman.

Either way, Omar had been instructed to secure the target one way or another. A live capture was preferred, but in no case was the intruder to escape with any information he—or she—had managed to acquire.

The members of Jamalzadah's contingent were equipped with various Kalashnikov rifles, captured from Red Army invaders during the decade between 1979 and '89 or purchased later from black-market dealers. In addition to those classics, they'd also acquired a few FN SCAR weapons: Fabrique Nationale Herstal's Special Operations Forces Combat Assault Rifle, designed in Belgium and sold worldwide, liberated from captured or dead Crusaders since 2009.

The SCARs weighed nearly seven pounds and measured thirty-one inches with their ten-inch folding stocks extended. Chambered for 5.56×45mm NATO rounds, they accepted twenty- and thirty-round STANAG box magazines, boasting an auto-fire rate of 650 rounds per minute with an effective range of 330 yards using standard iron sights—a range improved with addition of various scopes.

A few of the *talibés*, like Omar, also carried "Strike One" 9mm Parabellum pistols, Italian weapons also manufactured under license in Russia, where they were nicknamed *Strizh*, meaning "swift bird". Like the more famous Glocks, most of the Strike One's frame was made from polymer, holding the semiauto's weight at 1.65 pounds. And as with the Glock 17, each magazine held seventeen rounds, plus one in the spout.

All that, but the weapon Omar Jamalzadah wished most

to employ hung at his left hip, in a leather scabbard. It was a kukri knife from Nepal, favored by Gurkha warriors who all vowed that, having drawn the knife in combat, they would not return it to its sheath without a taste of blood. The kukri's thick, curved blade was made for chopping, with a penetrative force disproportional to its length. It thus inflicts deep wounds and penetrates resistant bone.

It should be perfect, Omar thought, for lopping off the head of their intended captive while a videographer captured the scene and broadcast it worldwide.

Whether his enemy was male or female meant no more to Jamalzadah than the gender of an insect crushed beneath his hiking boots—although, if truth be told, beheading faithless women was a fantasy he'd harbored from his youth, a fantasy yet unfulfilled.

But soon, perhaps. Maybe even tonight.

Bamyan Province

"Omar Jamalzadah believes he's getting closer," said Sediq Qayoumi. He sounded pleased.

Mohammed Ali Isani did not recognize the name, no reason why he should, but he assumed the man must be one of Qayoumi's underlings, assigned to hunt the fugitive they now believed to be American.

"What makes him think so?" asked Isani.

Sediq seemed about to take offense but managed to control

it. Rather than answering Isani's question, he replied, "I trust his judgment."

"That's all very well for you. But why should I? Why should my director-general, much less the Minister of National Defense?"

"If you must know—"

Isani cut him short. "I must. Consider it essential to our ongoing collaboration."

"In that case, we have information from a villager in Baghlan Province that a group of parachutists landed there within the past hour."

"And you have confirmation of that sighting?"

"Through an army source," Sediq replied. "Regular troops retrieved the parachutes and are engaged in searching for the infiltrators as we speak."

"But you expect to find them first?"

"It is my hope."

"Ah, hope. That often proves to be ephemeral."

"At present, we have the advantage. It appears the army's searchers have encountered certain difficulties in discovering the parachutists' trail."

"What difficulties?"

"Harsh terrain…and possibly some misdirection from our friends in the vicinity."

"Go on."

"The new arrivals have been spotted heading northward, while Kabul's troops are at present moving eastward, in response to what Americans might call a 'hot tip'."

"If the diversion proves successful, I commend you."

"Thank you. We—"

"But only if it leads to capture of the spy we seek. Without that, all your efforts have been wasted."

"I expect our men to be successful."

"And I hope you are correct, Sediq. But expectations, in their way, are fragile things. Like hope."

"We have, of course, invoked assistance from Allah."

Isani did his best to keep from smirking. Outwardly a true believer, raised on the Quran's teachings and strictures of Islamic law, he nonetheless trusted primarily in human will and in firepower.

"No doubt," he replied, "Allah has heard your supplications and shall find time to consider them. Unfortunately, time is something that we cannot spare. You say the infiltrators are proceeding northward in Baghlan Province."

Although Isani did not phrase the comment as a question, Sediq rushed to answer him. "That is correct, although their destination is as yet unclear."

"As yet." Isani let the words lie there between them as he scanned a mental map of the terrain in question. "North of Baghlan we have Kunduz Province, then."

"Or Takhar," Qayoumi said. "Depending on the route selected."

"Both of which abut Uzbekistan."

Sediq blinked once before he said, "Of course! The only country in the region still on speaking terms with the Crusaders, other than Ashraf Ghani's lapdogs in Kabul."

Mohammad Ashraf Ghani Ahmadzai, current president of so-called Afghani Islamic Republic, was indeed a traitor to his homeland and religion in the eyes of loyal jihadists. Deemed "progressive" by the heathen West, he had been Finance Minister before a losing presidential race back in 2009, then triumphed five years later with assistance from the Afghan military—and, no doubt, the CIA. He claimed to be the "president of all Afghans", asserting that his "heart breaks for the Talibans", yet he continued to abide Crusaders on his native soil and join in armed suppression of Allah's guerillas.

"If the spy escapes into Uzbekistan," Isani said, "there will be untold consequences. Who knows what information he—or she—may presently possess?"

"I count on speedy resolution of the problem," said Sediq.

"Don't count on it," Captain Isani said. "But rather, make it so."

Baghlan Province

"This here's far as we go," the Black Hawk pilot told Jack Cody, speaking to him through the earphones that reduced the helicopter's roar of sound to distant thunder. "Orders are, from here you're on your own."

Checking his GPS transponder to confirm coordinates, Jack thought, *That's how I like it,* then he gave the pilot a thumbs-up as the chopper began its steep descent. He shed the earphones, not quite wincing as the Black Hawk's thrumming engines nearly deafened him.

Touchdown was fleeting, lasting only long enough for Jack to leap clear of the open bay and scuttle in a crouch beyond the whirlwind generated by the rotors whirling overhead. Once he was clear, there was no point to looking back. He heard the chopper lifting off, banking away from him, returning southward to the sprawl of Hamid Karzai International. A storm of desert grit peppered his back but spared Jack's narrowed eyes.

Call it three-quarters of a mile to go on foot, and were men of SEAL Team X also approaching Sara's last known point of reference? Cody had no plan to connect with them—likely resulting in a firefight rather than cozy collaboration—but if they were somewhere up ahead of him, perhaps already bundling Sara up to get her off Afghan soil, he would have liked to know about it.

As it was...

Too late for second-guessing now. Whatever happened in the next half-hour, give or take, he'd chalk it up to fate, chance, luck, whatever. All he knew, right now, was that he'd signed on for the only kind of mission he still took these days.

One with the prospect that he'd wind up in a box—or, given where he was, more likely as a late-night snack for roving caracals, foxes, or jackals.

Step right up. First come, first served.

That prospect didn't bother Cody, since he cherished no hope for an afterlife. It would have pleased him to believe his wife and children were secure and happy somewhere, maybe in some alternate dimension where they'd never felt the agony of being murdered, but he placed no faith in fantasies of disembodied souls lounging on clouds and strumming harps.

As far as Cody was concerned, NASA had put that fairy tale to bed decades before his birth. There might be life somewhere in outer space, but he'd have bet the farm that any angels sporting halos would have been spotted by astronauts or long-range satellites by now.

And as for Hell, he figured nothing could be worse than what mankind inflicted on itself year-round, 24/7 in the waking world of hard and fast reality.

Right now, he had one goal and only one: to find Sara Durell if she was still in-country, do whatever he could manage toward her rescue if the men of SEAL Team X fell short, and get her out of the bizarre, chaotic no-man's land known as Afghanistan.

Cody had done time here already, plus his tours in Iraq, and all that he'd accomplished was to leave his precious family alone, defenseless against enemies at home. No matter how many opponents he had slain since then, the task of breaking even was eternally beyond him.

Only death would ultimately soothe his pain. Darkness beyond remembering.

But not tonight, if Jack could help it.

Here and now, he had a job to do, and it was shaping up to be a stone-cold grind. If he missed Sara and the SEALs whisked her away, he'd have a long walk waiting for him to the border of Uzbekistan. The odds of getting out alive weren't great, but that was as per usual.

For now, he'd take the journey one step at a time, and Heaven help whoever tried to bar his way.

"Confirm coordinates," MCPO Austin half-whispered to his point man/navigator, CPO Dakota Webster.

Webster keyed his own transponder—every man on SEAL Team X equipped with one, in case they should be separated—and replied, "Confirmed, Chief," rattling off the numbers all of them had now committed to their memories.

"I don't see anything so far," Austin observed. "Do you?"

"Squat," Webster said. "I'd say we have to risk the signal."

Austin frowned at that but realized there was no way around it. Contact was required, and he wasn't about to stroll around the Afghan desert shouting, waiting for their mission's subject to respond.

Without another word, Austin removed an Ultra E-17 tactical flashlight from a cargo pocket of his pants, cupping the light in his palm. Made of aircraft-grade aluminum, the Ultra E-17 could lengthen with a tug from 5.3 to 6.1 inches in length. Its convex lens covered a cluster of SM-L TX LED beads with a lamp life of 100,000 hours, with five modes including high, medium, low, strobe and SOS. Its white beam varied from 3,800 to 4,200 lumens, visible on high beam to 1,080 yards out.

Just what Austin required for winking at the Afghan night and waiting for his contact to respond.

He angled the flashlight northward, set its beam on

high-power and used his thumb to tap out Morse code dots and dashes translating to "Seeking contact. Please respond." Before he could repeat the message, Austin saw a pale light winking in the night responding, "Here. Identify."

They'd never actually been in touch and had no passwords to exchange. MCPO Austin settled for blinking out the silent message: "SEAL Team X."

A moment later, his sharp eyes picked out the terse reply. "Affirmative. Come over."

Hesitating, Austin huddled with the other members of his team, all versed in reading Morse from early training. All he asked them now was, "Any thoughts?"

"We've come this far," said PO3 Takazi. "Can't just turn around and bag it now."

"You got that right," said PO1 Swenson. "We're walking out, regardless, and that means we're heading north."

"I'll cover you from here," said Barnes, their designated marksman with the Barrett Light Fifty. "Somebody tries to move on you, I'll waste their ass."

"Okay," Austin replied. "I'll lead with half the team, the rest of you stay put until I call you up. On me, Shugari, Petri and Monsoor. First sign of any monkey business, light 'em up."

The men staying behind acknowledged Austin's order with a single voice and went to ground, the Barrett and their M4A1 carbines locked onto the last point where they'd seen their contact's flashlight winking in response to Austin's. Coming with him, Monsoor had the semi-auto twelve-gauge. Austin, Petri and Shugari had their own M4A1s, two of them underslung with M203 40mm launchers.

They had left nothing to chance, except a stroll through darkness, over hostile ground, to meet a person none of them had ever seen before.

And what could possibly go wrong?

The answer came back to him crystal-clear: just about anything.

Screw it, thought MCPO Austin. He had trained for this, had executed other covert missions without losing anybody from his team, all of them staged on deadly ground ranging from Syria and Lebanon, Angola and Somalia, on to the cocaine forests of Colombia and Paraguay. Austin had lost track of the men he'd put to sleep forever, focused on the job at hand and unconcerned with keeping score like some old Hollywood cowboy.

This job should be another feather in his cap, maybe another medal pinned to his dress uniform, unless—

He took another step, and suddenly the night caught fire.

CHAPTER 5

Sara Durell ducked automatically, instinctively, although the first shots weren't directed toward her hiding place amidst a pile of weathered boulders, mounded on the desert flats as if a dinosaur had come along and dropped its load during Jurassic times and left the heap to petrify.

It only took an instant for her mind to recognize that of the hostile guns—at least three dozen of them, firing in full-automatic mode—none were directed toward the spot where she was hunkered down. Their handlers had some target spotted on the desert flats southwest of her, no tracers loaded in their magazines, no telltale laser-sighting beams in Christmas colors.

All she saw was blinking muzzle flashes, guessing that at least some of the shooters must be using some kind of night-vision scopes or goggles, since a new moon overhead provided no spare light and spotty clouds were drawn across the desert's field of stars.

Worse yet, the guns were firing from both sides of her position, northwest and southeast, which told Sara she was pretty well surrounded.

How in hell had that happened?

She nearly flinched as someone in the down-range open darkness started to return fire from a couple of positions, telling her that they were spread out on the wasteland. Her first instinct was to join the fight, but she restrained herself, unsure which side—if either one—she should support.

The fighters in the open had to be her rescue party, right?

The time was spot on and she hadn't budged from the assigned coordinates since she'd received a message telling her that help was on the way and closing in. Now, from what Sara saw and heard, that rescue plan was literally being shot to hell and gone.

The cryptic messages she had received made it impossible to I.D. her intended saviors. Simply sending out a time and GPS coordinates was dangerous enough. No one at Langley or wherever would risk hinting if the pickup team was army, navy, air force, or a squad of mercenaries picked up on the fly, when they had spare time on their hands.

Or, then again, it might have nothing in the world to do with her.

Afghanistan had been an active war zone the U.S. invasion began, twenty-six days after 9/11 in 2001. Eighteen years and counting, America's longest-ever war, and what had been accomplished? Forget the upbeat network news at home. American soldiers kept dying, along with uncounted civilians and hostile Islamists. "Elected" government kept hanging by a thread, one shove away from toppling, and the only people coming out ahead were heroin producers, with their convoys covered by Afghani regulars and allied Western troops.

There was an outside chance—way, *way* outside, admittedly—that Sara was observing one more clash between the Taliban and Afghan National Army, maybe even troops from NATO's RSM—the "Resolute Support Mission"—but she wasn't much of a believer in bizarre coincidence.

There'd been no headlights cutting through the darkness, nothing to suggest a convoy moving north, loaded with opium, so that was out. No military vehicles advancing, not even the clip-clop echoes of a camel caravan.

No. Sara was convinced that what she saw before her now was her one hope of rescue going up in gun smoke. When an RPG rocket roared off across the flats and detonated in a fireball on impact, she had a fleeting glimpse of men in camouflage fatigues diving for cover, maybe some of them too late.

What could she do about it now?

Stand ready with her weapons if a target should present itself, an adversary come too close.

And maybe wish she still remembered how to pray.

MCPO Ben Austin was bleeding from a thigh wound, had applied a tourniquet while trading fire with whoever had ambushed SEAL Team X, while wondering if this would be his End of Days.

He wasn't married, was an only child, orphaned the same year he had joined the U.S. Navy, when his parents bought it in a rented car outside Orlando, on a trip to Disney World, and would leave no one grieving when he shuffled off the mortal coil.

In short, he was the perfect SEAL, but it was clear he'd screwed the pooch this time—or else, the enemy had been one jump ahead of him from the beginning, close to coming out atop a lethal game of cat-and-mouse.

He squeezed the trigger on his M203 launcher, sent a 40mm HE round arcing into the desert night, watching it blow on impact with the soil, perhaps inflicting wounds within 130 meters, though its sure-fire killing radius was only five.

He could have used an M583A1 Star Parachute Round to light the battleground, but what would be the point? His enemies would only turn it to their own advantage, picking out the members of his team as they were trying to conceal themselves with nothing much for cover on the flats.

How many of his men were even still alive?

A blast from PO2 Monsoor's shotgun told him one SEAL was still able to fight, and he'd already heard their sniper's Barrett Light Fifty sending .50-caliber rounds down range at half a mile per second.

Hitting who or what, if anyone or anything?

The other friendly fire was all from M4A1 carbines like his own, but there had been no time to count them, a chance for Austin to spot his people once the AK round had ripped into his leg and left him sprawling in the sand. He didn't think the slug had clipped his femoral artery—good news, as far as it went—but he was still bleeding despite the tourniquet and knew he couldn't leave that on indefinitely without compounding initial damage from his wound.

It wasn't MCPO Austin's first combat-related wound, but it was certainly his worst so far.

That *so far* almost made him laugh, considering the odds of getting through tonight alive, along with any of his men, were looking worse with each second that ticked away.

Unless they started kicking major ass and did it soon, he'd never get to meet the spook they'd been assigned to snatch out of harm's way.

"Fat lot of good that did," he muttered to himself, and fed another round into the breech-loading grenade launcher mounted beneath his carbine's barrel.

It was time to rock and roll—make that past time—if anyone from SEAL Team X was going to survive the night. They had to be alive in order to complete their mission, and he couldn't even think about their contact know, wherever he might be.

Already dead, perhaps? Or had insurgents captured him and forced him to divulge coordinates for their meeting? Would Langley or whoever have dispatched a spy who could withstand long-term interrogation be determined enemies? Was there any such person presently alive on Earth?

The only way to find out, Austin knew, was to fight on, break through the damned insurgents and complete the next phase of their orders.

What went down from then on would be anybody's guess.

Jack Cody liked to think he was prepared for anything, around the clock, in any situation, but the first outbreak of gunfire had surprised him, even so.

The good news: it was still a couple hundred yards ahead of him, about two football fields of open ground, with darkness cloaking him.

The bad news: stray bullets and ricochets could kill him just as easily as any round sent hurtling toward him by a sniper peering through a GEN-III OMNI-V–VII night-vision telescopic sight.

With that in mind, Cody proceeded in a fighting crouch, not quite a duck walk, still too far out from the action to start crawling on his belly through the sand and gravel. He could tell that there were two sides fighting, one outnumbered three or four to one by its opponents. Logic told him that the weaker side, in terms of numbers, ought to be the SEALs dispatched to help Sara Durell—which made the ambush party with the numbers on its side either jihadists from the Taliban or Kabul regulars who'd tangled with the rescue team somehow.

Was it deliberate? Had someone locked onto the SEALs somehow as they were parachuting in?

Jack knew that answering that question wouldn't help him in the least, so he dismissed it from his mind, continuing his forward progress toward the battleground.

A better question: had the SEALs been jumped before or after they linked up with Sara? Was she also huddled in the crossfire now, along with her intended rescuers? Had she been nabbed by enemies before the pickup team arrived on site?

Was she, perhaps, already dead?

That prospect got him moving faster, moving closer to a point roughly behind whoever still survived from SEAL Team X, with hostiles pouring automatic fire into the dark void from two sides, angling from the northwest and northeast. That left a dark dead zone between the two jihadist firing squads—and what could Cody make of that?

It had to be some kind of obstacle they either couldn't scale in time to spring their trap or else decided that it wasn't worth their effort. In the middle of the Afghan desert, that meant it was probably a hill or small mountain. Judged by height, a hill stood less than 2,300 hundred feet high, while mountains towered over them, the pinnacle of Everest sky-scraping at an altitude above 29,029 feet.

The fly in that theoretical ointment: neither hill nor mountain should exist at this location, based upon the topographic map Cody had memorized aboard the Black Hawk chopper out of Kabul. What remained, then, was one of the countless rocky outcroppings that marked the Afghan landscape much as pimples sprouted from the cheeks of acne sufferers.

And a rock pile of any size would make a primo hiding place for someone on the run—or waiting for delivery from hostile hands, back to her own home turf.

Again, it was another case of good news versus bad news.

On the upside, Jack thought he could say approximately where he'd find Sara, if she was still alive not captured yet.

The downside, simply stated: to approach her, Jack would either have to cross the killing ground with both sides firing at him, or else circle wide around the fight to east or west, and come in from behind Sara, approaching from the north.

Knowing Plan B would waste time that he couldn't spare, Cody moved forward, easing into Hell on Earth.

Omar Jamalzadah triggered a short burst from his FN SCAR assault rifle, one of the captured U.S. weapons he'd appropriated for himself from his *Sara Kheta* team's conglomerate arsenal, mouthed a silent prayer to Allah as he fired that his bullets would find and slay one of his enemies.

Sara Kheta teams—translated from Pashto to English as Danger Units or Red Units—were the Taliban's elite special forces, better armed and trained than regular insurgent units, typically employed against high-value targets or special offensives such as staging jailbreaks, terminating major sieges, capturing highly strategic areas, or guarding VIPs during their travels. In this case, the job was running down a fugitive Crusader and eliminating any foreign troops dispatched to aid in his (or her) escape.

Launched in December 2015, against rogue Islamic State rivals on Afghan soil, the *Sara Kheta* units not only got their pick of newer, better weapons and explosives, but also had first call on high-tech military gear including Russian-made

PNV-10T tactical night-vision goggles and 1PN58 night-vision telescopic rifle sights.

Both of those toys were helpful for tonight's wet work.

Scanning the battlefield, Jamalzadah observed that two of the invaders, almost certainly Americans dispatched by the Great Satan's Pentagon, were sprawled unmoving on the desert's killing floor. He couldn't swear that they were dead, but neither one had moved for minutes now, even when bullets kicked up dust and grit within a hand's width of their prostrate forms.

Two down and half a dozen left to go.

Which still left their intended contact unaccounted for.

He (or was it she, as Mohammed Isani had suggested?) was Omar's primary target and must not escape, no matter what befell the would-be rescuers now trapped and dying in their turn.

Jamalzadah knew that failure meant his own death was inevitable, likely via crucifixion and stoning. Decapitation was reserved for captured infidels, and while it raised a storm of outrage when displayed on social media, Omar knew that the carving knife was quicker and more merciful than slow and agonizing execution of a failure to the Holy Cause.

He'd seen men last for days, their arms and legs bound to a framework built from rusty scraps of pipe, finally dying from thirst or exposure, rather than the stones hurled at them by Afghani villagers at gunpoint urging from the Taliban.

There would be no such death for Omar Jamalzadah while he had a single round left for one of his weapons, and a finger strong enough to pull a trigger. He would rather meet God on his own terms and be done with it than leave that choice to men he'd once considered friends and his comrades-in-arms.

He found another target with his bulky NSPUM—the English acronym for Night Small-arms Scope Unified Modernized, from Russian—and spotted a Crusader trying to adjust a tourniquet he'd looped around one wounded thigh—and paused before delivering the long-range *coup de grâce*.

Instead of firing for the soldier's head or heart, Omar fixed his crosshairs upon the hand securing the tourniquet, squeezed off, and saw his bullets shred that hand, shearing its fingers off and ripping through the limb already wounded by some other rifleman from his Red Unit.

This time, when the damned crusader toppled over backwards, lips writing with curses Omar could not hear, he'd lost ability and will to stanch the blood tide pumping from below.

As the American surrendered to his fate, Omar tracked past him with the NSPUM scope. Seeking another target and another until all of them were stone-cold dead and only one stray enemy remained.

The first thing PO2 Travis Monsoor had learned in Navy SEAL training was perseverance. Never, under any circumstances, just give up and quit, regardless of the odds against him or how hopeless they appeared.

But for the first time since he's graduated as a full-fledged SEAL, Monsoor was questioning that sage advice.

So far, Monsoor had seen four members of his team go down and figured all of them were dead or on their way across that point of no return. They weren't moving, had stopped making the normal sounds of wounded men, and gave no other signs of life.

That was the shits, all right. Since being formed into the unit known as SEAL Team X, they'd only lost one man, and that was to a training accident. That one, Chuck Osborne, was replaced by Kyle Swenson before their first real mission in the field and they had gotten over that the same way they'd endured whatever else went down, starting on day one in boot camp.

But now...

Swenson was definitely dead, head shot, along with team commander Austin, CPO Webster, and PO3 Takazi. Monsoor couldn't see the other three from where he'd gone to ground, but none of them were answering his Blue Tooth shout-outs to the night, and that was worrisome.

Worse yet was the idea, edging toward certainty under the present circumstances, that they'd failed to carry out the job assigned to them.

One thing Monsoor didn't have to think about right now was facing up to that failure long-term.

Bruised feelings, tarnished honor—none of that shit mattered after you were dead.

Did it?

A scuttling movement in the desert darkness, coupled with a slacking-off of hostile fire, alerted him to enemies approaching. He was cut off and surrounded now, but there was still some fight left in Travis Monsoor, as the jihadists were about to learn.

The first rule of a Navy SEAL was no man left behind, if there was any way on Earth to bring him out, alive or otherwise.

The second rule was the flip side of Number One: never let the *hajis* capture you alive.

Better to bite the literal bullet than to suffer days of torture in the guise of questioning, then wind up being slaughtered on one of those videos that popped up periodically on Facebook, Instagram, wherever.

Rudyard Kipling nailed it down more than a hundred years ago, the only poem offered up in Navy SEAL training and duly memorized. Its title was "The Young British Soldier," and the pertinent stanza declaimed in Cockney slang:

When you're wounded and left on Afghanistan's plains,
And the women come out to cut up what remains,
Jest roll to your rifle and blow out your brains
An' go to your Gawd like a soldier.

Rifle, shotgun, or HK45CT pistol—it all came out the same.

But first...

Monsoor unclipped one of his M61 frag grenades and pulled the pin, together with its extra safety dubbed a "jungle clip" that kept the pin from snagging on the obstacles of heavy vegetation and producing lethal accidents. Once Monsoor had released the safety lever—aka the "spoon"—he'd have four to five seconds left before the M204-series Timed Friction Fuse burned down to doomsday.

And that iffy extra second could mean all the difference between survival and extinction.

Monsoor pitched the grenade overhand, toward the scraping sounds made by his enemies. Before it blew and lit them up, he had the M4 Super 90 shotgun braced against his shoulder, aimed down range, loaded with eight founds of double-aught buckshot.

When he saw his adversaries briefly backlit by the HE blast down range, Monsoor spotted the ones still on their feet and moving forward, rapid-firing into them, trusting the shot's spread to wreak havoc even if he didn't see them drop.

Four rounds, and then another burst of four, exhausting the Benelli's load. There was no time to feed the magazine fresh cartridges, so Monsoor let the shotgun drop and pulled his .45. Ten rounds plus one—the one he had to save for last, to go out like a soldier.

Sighting down the pistol's slide at shadows in the night, he shouted, "Come and get it while its hot, you sons of bitches!"

And they came.

Sara Durell huddled in darkness, smelling blood and cordite, watching as the last of her intended rescuers went down, riddled with slugs from various Kalashnikovs. She held her own weapon, ready to sell her life at a steep price, determined as the Navy SEALs had been to skip the horrors of captivity with members of the Taliban.

Dying was one thing, but the grim preliminaries leading up to it were something else.

And Sara knew damned well that as a female prisoner of war in Muslim hands, she'd suffer more than any captured man.

Well, more than any man except the U.S. President, perhaps, and he would no more wind up in jihadist hands than he'd go golfing on the moons of Jupiter next weekend.

A sudden, deathly stillness settled over the Afghani desert. From her elevated vantage point, scanning the field below through ESS 740 night-vision goggles, she watched survivors of the ambush party checking corpses of their enemies before they paid attention to their dead and wounded comrades.

Good news on that front, if a sane mind could apply the term. None of the SEALs now being kicked and poked by bayonets would face interrogation. All of them were down and out for good.

At times like this, stray thoughts arrived unbidden. How would eight deaths be explained to family and friends back home? Was the fiasco Sara's fault, for nearly being caught while on surveillance of the Taliban? Was she responsible for Roland's death the night a sentry had surprised them at their task?

Counterproductive, she decided. *Let it go.*

She wouldn't—couldn't—travel down that dead-end rabbit hole of self-recrimination. Everyone who'd died so far over the past two days on her behalf, both friends and enemies, had acted under orders, willingly. There was no point in second-guessing anything she couldn't change.

And would there be a follow-up attempt to pull her out, return her to a modicum of safety somewhere distant from the hellhole of Afghanistan?

Unlikely, in her estimation. Not impossible, but...

Something hissed behind her, not reptilian, more like a person seeking her attention without using spoken words. Not something she'd expect a warrior of the Taliban to do, when he could simply shoot her in the back of shout at her to drop her weapon, raise her empty hand.

"Not freaking likely," Sara muttered to herself, and spun around, her automatic carbine leveled from the hip.

"Who, now!" a man half-whispered from the shadows. "Not so hasty."

Struggling to mask her shock, Sara made out his form, rifle in hand, and nearly gasped.

"Cody?"

"None other," Jack replied. "Surprised to see me?"

"What the hell—"

He cut her question short. "What say we get away from here before we have that chat?"

"You have someplace in mind?" she asked.

"I'm thinking we head north. Agreed?"

"The Uzbek border."

"Roger that."

"It may not be as easy as you make it sound. Slipping away from here, I mean."

"Between the two of us, I figure we can pull it off."

"Or die trying?"

"There's always that," he granted, with a smile.

"Okay. How did you plan to do this?"

"One step at a time," Jack said. "They're busy checking out the SEALs right now. We should start making tracks before they're done."

"They have night-vision gear," Sara reminded him.

"And we do, too." Jack reached into one of his many pockets and retrieved a pair of goggles similar in size and form to Sara's own.

"All right, then," she conceded. "After you."

They made it down the backside of the desert rock pile, facing northward into nothingness. From where they stood, Jack estimated that the Afghan-Uzbek border must be right around 130 miles away. Walking nonstop around the clock, on level ground devoid of any obstacles or opposition, healthy people living in a perfect world might covering that distance in forty-three to forty-five hours, depending on their size and stride.

Now work the variables. He and Sara both were fit, well trained and capable. That said, Jack knew they'd likely have to hide out during daylight hours to avoid hostile patrols, perhaps including skyborne searchers from the Afghan Air Force, flying fixed-wing planes made in America or Russian helicopter gunships furnished following a decent interval after the Soviet withdrawal back in 1989. Toss in the Taliban, whose Red Squads would be searching high and low until they'd run their prey to ground.

Even the country, without human hunters on their trail, ranked as an enemy. Afghan desert broils by day, freezes at night, and teems with wildlife that includes a wide variety of predators: wild cats including leopards, cheetahs, assorted smaller breeds; jackals and wolves; black bears; nine species of eagles; cobras and kraits, with half a dozen vipers in the mix; and top that off with scorpions, tarantulas, black widows.

Still the worst threat came from human beings.

Moving silently across the flats with Sara at his heels, Jack didn't even want to think about the Uzbek border crossing yet. It was too far away and fraught with perils of its own.

Sufficient unto this day was the evil heaped upon his plate.

CHAPTER 6

Washington, D.C.

It took a beat for Denham Boyd to recognize the sat phone's chirping from the his lower-right-hand desk drawer, where the instrument was out of sight but seldom out of mind. He reached it on the second chirp and took the call.

"Tell me."

"You want the bad news or the good news first?" Jack Cody asked from half a world away.

"Your call," Boyd answered.

"The bad news, then. That tour you booked fell through."

Jack playing cagey, even on a scrambled line that ricocheted to Boyd's office from outer space.

"What happened?" Boyd inquired.

"They've all come down with something," Cody said.

"How bad?"

"The worst."

Meaning they'd lost eight Navy SEALs, an all-time record for a single mission since the program had been launched by JFK in 1962.

"That *is* bad news. I'll have to pass it on."

"Good luck with that."

"You mentioned good news?"

"Right. I've got the package that we talked about."

Boyd let another second pass before he spoke again, then asked, "Is it intact?"

"Hang on."

Eight and a half hours ahead of Eastern Standard Time, a phone changed hands. The next voice on the line was one that Boyd had nearly given up on hearing this side of the rumored afterlife.

"It's me," Sara Durell confirmed.

"And you're okay?"

"The best you could expect."

"Sorry about that other thing," Boyd said, keeping it vague despite the line's encryption.

"Which one?" Sara asked.

He had to think about it for a second, realizing she'd had two grim losses in as many days: first, her hand-picked interpreter, and now the men of SEAL Team X.

"Both, actually," Boyd replied.

"Expecting static from upstairs."

She didn't phrase it as a question, so he didn't bother answering. Of course, the president would be pissed off. Would he be furious enough to fire Boyd on the spot? Doubtful, but nothing that had happened in the past two days would auger well for job security.

"About that other thing…"

"You should have had my last transmission dump."

"Affirmative. It was…surprising."

"That's an understatement."

"Well, the company we work for *is* conservative."

"I hear you."

"A response is in the works."

"Okay," she answered cautiously. "You understand there's nothing I can do about it now, from this end."

"No, that's fine. We've got coordinates from what you sent before. Looks like we'll book them for a cruise."

And more than one, if what he'd heard so far was true.

Cruise missiles, that would be. Categorized by size, speed (subsonic or supersonic), and range (twenty-five to twenty-five hundred kilometers), the missiles may be launched from land-based platforms, aircraft, surface ships or submarines. Guidance systems vary widely. Payloads range from conventional high explosives to nuclear warheads.

In the present case, the White House and Joint Chiefs of Staff were thinking ship-based launches from the Persian Gulf, flying on non-ballistic, extremely low-altitude trajectories. Multiple targets would include some of the largest Afghan opium plantations and a factory in Taliban-held territory where jihadi scientists were cranking out their toxic "Devil's Rain".

Granted, blowing the factory to bits might spread the gas

around, but Boyd wasn't concerned about Afghanis who supported and protected Taliban insurgents. Neither, he suspected, was the President of the United States or anyone drawing a Pentagon paycheck.

"That ought to do it," Sara told him.

"Fingers crossed. When are you coming home?"

"No ETA available so far. We've been distracted by a nature walk."

"I can reach out and try to smooth things for you at the border."

"We'd appreciate it," she replied. No point in mentioning which border, on the off chance that security might have a glitch somewhere along the line.

"I'll get right on it."

"Roger that."

She cut the distant link and left Boyd with dead air humming in his left ear. He killed the sat phone, tucked it back into its desk-drawer charging cradle, and considered how much he could safely tell The Man.

Baghlan Province

Sara and Jack ran out of night when they had only covered ten miles and a bit, both weary from the forced march over hostile turf. A long-abandoned mine shaft offered sanctuary as dawn broke along the eastern skyline, still a brisk hike from the point where they would have to choose between Kunduz and Takhar Provinces for their push onward to Uzbekistan.

They hadn't talked much on the trail, couldn't afford to waste their breath or miss potential danger signs along the way, but it was different inside the musty shaft, once they had checked it out for dangerous wildlife. Now, over MREs—buffalo chicken for Brody, with cornbread stuffing; penne pasta with sausage and Mexican rice for Durell—they settled down to hash it out, their weapons lying close at hand.

"How did he take it?" Jack inquired.

"About the way you would expect."

"That well?"

"They're sending out cruise missiles. Might be airborne as we speak."

"That could distract our trackers," he suggested.

"Could. Or just might kick the hornet's nest."

"That, too."

She didn't have to ask how far they'd come or how much farther they had left to go. Aside from GPS coordinates, both Jack and Sara had pedometers that ticked off mileage as they walked, not just for mall walkers and urban joggers anymore.

It still remained a tossup as to which northern Afghani province they'd traverse to reach the border with Uzbekistan, but whichever they decided on, they'd still need help getting across. The border between nations spanned 203 miles east to west, between the Afghan borders with Tajikistan and Turkmenistan. Since 2001 every foot of that border had been barred to travelers by a normal barbed wire fence and a second, taller barbed wire barrier that pulsed nonstop with 380 volts of electricity. Besides the dual fences, there were land mines and heavily armed Uzbek soldiers with leashed attack dogs.

In fact, only one other frontier on Earth—the border between North and South Korea—was more heavily guarded today.

The only authorized crossing point lies at Termez–Hairatan on the northbound road from Mazār-i-Sharīf, the capital of Balkh Province and fourth-largest city in Afghanistan. Guards on the Afghan side are normally laid-back and amenable to bribes, while their Uzbek counterparts demand immigration forms filled out in duplicate, while searching luggage, closely scrutinizing cell phones, laptops and cameras for anything deemed pornographic or otherwise suspect. Islamic guards take pride in striking blows for both morality and national security, constantly alert for photos of nude women, public buildings, aircraft, ships and other vehicles, or troops in uniform.

Trying to cross the border with a weapon—knife, gun, or whatever—just might get you killed.

"You have a plan worked out for crossing over?" Cody asked, as they were finishing their meals, before they started digging holes to plant the plastic bags and other leftovers.

"If I'd connected with the SEALs," Sara replied, "they were supposed to call in air support and drop me off at Tashkent International. From there, I should have caught Uzbekistan Airways to Tokyo Narita, then picked up Delta to Atlanta, and back home to Washington from there."

"Around the world in eighty ways," he quipped.

"Instead of hiking back and hoping we can pass the border checkpoint without being shot or jailed."

"I call that living on the edge."

"As long as we're still living when it's done, and preferably not inside a prison cell."

"I'll cover you as best I can," Cody replied. "But truth be told, I'm in no mood to let them put me in a cage."

"There's a surprise. Still playing hardball."

"It's the only game in town," Jack said.

"Meaning the only one you'll sign up for," Sara corrected him. "Still hoping somebody will cast you for a remake of *The Wild Bunch* after fifty years?"

"Hey, everybody needs a goal."

"Another Western, then. What was it Josey Wales said to the bounty hunter in that jerkwater saloon?"

" 'Dyin' ain't much of a living, boy'."

"Take it to heart, Jack."

"What heart?"

"I have faith it's in there, somewhere."

"I'll take that bet," he said. "And first watch, too."

Bamyan Province

"I assume you've heard the news," Captain Isani said.

"I have," Sediq Qayoumi answered with a rueful tone.

"I must communicate within the hour to my major who, it's safe to say, will not be overjoyed."

"You think I am?" Qayoumi challenged. The Afghani's tone had gone from sullen, almost to combative in the time it took to draw a single breath.

Isani forged ahead as if Sediq had not spoken. "My problem now," he said, "is to present the information without casting it in terms of utter failure and humiliation."

"Meaning that you plan on blaming me, presumably?"

"Who else would you suggest should bear responsibility?"

"For all I know, the leak was on your side. The whole world knows that ISI headquarters is a sieve."

Isani took a deep breath, held it briefly, striving to control the temper that was heating up his cheeks. "Suppose you are correct," he said at last. "If someone leaked the information from Islamabad, why would the spies have crept around outside your headquarters and killed one of your guards? Why are the missiles only falling now, instead of last week or last month?"

Qayoumi clearly could not answer that. Instead, he sat and glared across Isani's desk.

"Very well," Isani said after a pregnant pause. "Since we're agreed on fault, what can we do to remedy the situation, if indeed there may be anything?"

Qayoumi asked, "Where have the missiles struck so far?"

"It would be easier to say where they have not," Isani answered back. "The factory outside Sheberghan, of course, was first to go. Our comrades in Turkmenistan are none too pleased with the direction of prevailing winds."

Sheberghan was the capital of Jowzjan Province, in the far north of Afghanistan, adjacent to the Turkmen border. Both nations espoused Islam and enjoyed economic collaboration, epitomized since 2015 by construction of the Trans-Afghanistan Pipeline bearing natural gas and a major Turkmen railroad facilitating fuel exports. Turkmenistan was also a transshipment point for Afghan drugs en route to Russia and Europe, ignored under the 1995 Turkmen declaration of "permanent neutrality". Israel had opened an embassy in Ashgabat six years ago, but with Turkmenistan's population 94 percent Muslim, President Gurbanguly Berdimuhamedow's support for Tel Aviv was little more than lip service.

"The Devil's Rain has crossed the border, then?" Qayoumi asked.

"Assisted by southerly winds as we speak. Our friends, if we may still consider them as such, are pleased to act surprised, but that will soon turn into 'outrage'."

"And the rest?"

"Incendiary strikes so far on opium plantations in the provinces of Farah and Nimruz, doubtless with more to come."

Both men knew the statistics. Afghanistan produced 93 percent of the planet's non-pharmaceutical-grade opiates, 95 percent of Europe's illegal heroin, and also ranked as world's leading producer of hashish. Primary opium cultivation was centered in Farah and Nimruz Provinces, to the southwest, and in the eastern provinces of Kabul and Nangarhar, abutting Pakistan. Narcotics contributed 52 percent of Afghanistan's GNP—$2.7 billion yearly, on average—and supported some 400,000 jobs, more than the combined Afghan National Security Forces.

"This could not have been foretold, Captain," Qayoumi said.

"I beg to differ. It was perfectly predictable the moment that your men allowed the spy to slip away from them. And now, it seems they've failed a second time."

"We will—"

"Enough!" Isani cut him off. "The only question still remaining now is whether you can fix the mess you've made, or I shall have to do it personally, over your dead body."

Baghlan Province

"Yes, sir. Certainly. I understand." Omar Jamalzadah cut the sat phone link and passed it back to Nelufar Kadim, his second in command.

"Was he not pleased?" Kadim inquired.

"Pleased?" It was all Omar could do to keep from snorting out a bitter laugh.

"Yes, sir. With the elimination of eight US soldiers. Was it not a victory to celebrate?"

Jamalzadah faced Kadim with a scowl. "I would not call it celebration, Nelufar. The terms 'incompetence' and 'failure' were employed, along with 'idiocy'. I believe that fairly sums it up."

"But, sir—"

"By Allah's beard, the *spy* is all that matters. Don't you understand that yet? It does not matter if we kill a hundred soldiers, or a thousand, if the goddamned spy escapes!"

"Forgive me, sir."

"There shall be no forgiveness, Nelufar, for any of us, if we do not rectify this 'hideous embarrassment'. That is another phrase that I neglected to include in my description of our lord and master's celebration."

"Sir—"

"We are to seek our enemy, the only one who matters, somewhere to the north. I'm told that he—or *she*, if you can credit that—will seek asylum in Uzbekistan."

Kadim blinked upon hearing that. "But, sir—"

"I know," Jamalzadah talked over him again. "We have no way of knowing where a border crossing may occur, somewhere along eighty-five miles of frontier spanning two Afghan provinces."

"It seems impossible," Kadim replied.

"Yet there is hope. Our prey is traveling on foot, while we are not. And we have one more edge over the stinking infidel."

"You mean...?"

"I do," Omar replied. "Prepare the drones."

Baghlan Province

Sara Durell was tired of hiding in the mine shaft, but she'd suffered worse—far worse—on other missions in the field and could accommodate discomfort as required. It felt strange to her, being in close quarters with Jack Cody, but she hadn't yet decided whether that was good or bad strange.

So far, it just felt *different*. And it was keeping them alive, at least in the short term.

"You hear that?" Cody asked, distracting Sara from her private reverie.

"Hear what?"

"Listen."

He shifted closer to the old mine's adit and she followed him, moving with a cat burglar's stealth and carrying her short Kalashnikov carbine. They stopped short of stepping into sunlight, Cody standing with his head cocked, index finger pointing skyward.

"There," he said.

And Sara heard the not-too-distant buzzing sound. "Is that—?"

Jack beat her to the punchline. "It's a drone, unless I miss my guess."

But clearly not a Predator. Those typically flew around twenty thousand feet and were inaudible at ground level, at least until their Hellfire missiles started raining down. Conversely, smaller private drones—many equipped with cameras and/or heat-seeking surveillance devices—were ubiquitous these days, worldwide. Amazon offered various models online ranging upward from $28 plus shipping, with the more sophisticated models topping out around $300. Paparazzi used them now to stalk celebrities, while governments had found it necessary to announce airspace restrictions on drone flights around their "sensitive" facilities.

Aside from DIY surveillance gear, civilian drones could also carry other payloads, up to and including high explosive charges for the techno-nerds who had a special axe to grind. In January 2018 one had crashed onto the White House lawn, unseen by Secret Service personnel until it dropped out of the sky. Elsewhere, felons were using drones in various capacities: for smuggling contraband across borders, hacking into computers and home security systems, decoying police, intimidating adversaries or prospective witnesses, and plotting jailbreaks.

Eyes in the sky were the wave of today. How could the Taliban, with all its drug money on tap, fail to climb aboard the trend?

"We're safe from it in here," Sara observed.

"Until we move outside," Jack said. "Unless you plan on staying put, that is."

She knew he had a point. With infrared technology, a drone could spot them moving over open ground at any time of day or night. Even if they could spot it, bring it tumbling down, that fact alone would pinpoint their location when the drone lost contact with its handler. And that wouldn't guarantee her trackers didn't have multiple flying eyes in service, backing one another up.

"Good thing it's noisy, then," she offered.

"That won't help us knock it down at night."

He had a point, as usual. While both of them carried night-vision gear, its range was limited in terms of scanning open nighttime skies. It couldn't take the place of radar, and their long guns lacked the range to drop most drones, even the smaller ones, assuming she or Jack could zero on one of the flitting, flying targets.

"So, we keep our fingers crossed," she said.

"As long as that won't interfere with pulling triggers," Jack replied.

"When did it ever?"

Overhead, the humming airborne engine sound was fading into distance as the drone—or whatever it was—moved on. She let herself relax a bit, but not too much. They still had far to go, through territory overrun with enemies and no prospect of any further help dispatched from Washington or Langley.

Not that the attempt to rescue her last night had been a "help" in any sense. The effort was sincere enough, but it had cost the lives of eight brave men and must have helped her adversaries zero in on where their hunt for her should concentrate.

Now, she had Jack, and that left Sara with mixed feelings.

She admired him on the one hand, even though he pushed the envelope on every mission he performed on her behalf, a man who—like fabled gunman-dentist John "Doc" Holliday of old—seemed literally not to care whether he lived or died. So far, he had performed each task assigned to him and left a trail of bodies in his wake, apparently without a vestige of remorse.

She trusted Cody with her life, but was that wise if he

could not be trusted with his own?

As for the visceral attraction Sara felt for Jack...well, that would be a subject for some future time, she thought. Always assuming they still had a future left.

Jack Cody sat a few feet back into the long-abandoned mine, invisible to any spotters overhead, concealed by shadows from the sunbaked Afghan desert stretching out in front of him to east and north.

He sipped a little water from his MOLLE pack's three-liter hydration unit, just two swallows, calculating how much farther he could travel without stopping to refill the pouch, and whether that would even be an option. Sara had been stuck in-country for at least a day longer than Jack had and he guessed she must be running low on water even now.

Something to think about when they could leave their hidey-hole and pick up with their northward trek where they'd left off at sunrise.

If their enemies hadn't arrived by then to root them out.

Jack knew it would be difficult for anyone to sneak up on them during daylight—and impossible if they were using motor vehicles—but he and Sara *could* be trapped inside the played-out mine without great difficulty. Should their enemies appear, Jack knew they couldn't run for it, exposed on open ground, without being cut down in seconds flat.

As for the mine itself, the deep shaft could become their tomb if they were cut off from the outside world. A small squad—hell, maybe a single rifleman—could pen them up inside while reinforcements gathered, cutting off escape. From that point on, the enemy could try to flush them out with gunfire, flamethrowers, or some variety of gas, even the rumored "Devil's Rain" itself. Should all else fail, a satchel charge or small bundle of dynamite would seal the mine till kingdom come, trapping its occupants forever in the dark.

Of course, there might be exit shafts somewhere, but finding one before their flashlights died was a slim hope at best, and if they reached the surface there would still be countless guns to face. A rancid version of fresh air might find its way into the mind through ventilation shafts, but breathing would become superfluous once Jack and Sara ran out of water and food.

Survival experts claimed an "average" person could survive four to six weeks without food while they wasted away, but hydration was critical. The lyric phrase "How Dry I Am" was meant to be a Prohibition era joke—part of a longer ditty titled "The Near Future", penned in 1919—but in fact, a person barred from access to water might die within a week, faster depending on ambient heat, exertion, and the victim's body mass index before they lost access to liquids.

Bad news, for someone who was pledged to tough it out and die the hard way, as a shriveled husk of skin and bones. Cody, for his part, had no fear of engendered by religion or societal mores of checking out before his time had theoretically elapsed. An hour hadn't passed without considering that option, since his wife and children were annihilated in an act of terrorism.

But the suicide solution didn't suit him. Not yet, anyway.

A world of enemies lay waiting for him to confront them, risk his life while trying to end theirs, and so far he'd been more than equal to the task. As for today, maybe tomorrow… well, he took each hour as it came, with no pipe dreams about a rosy future waiting for him in the by-and-by.

Almost unconsciously, he reached out for his AK-107, lying close beside him on the mine shaft's rocky floor, worn smooth over the years by boots, wheelbarrows and ore carts. The feel of it was reassuring to him now, an object that he recognized and trusted in a world where very little else could be relied upon.

Guns usually worked if you maintained them properly. The sun came up at dawn and disappeared at dusk, as it had always done.

And everybody died when their time rolled around, like it or not.

Jack would be ready for it, and he planned on taking out as many rotten bastards as he could when that time came.

But if he could help Sara in the meantime, maybe even get her out of this predicament, why not?

Baghlan Province

"Certainly, I understand." Omar Jamalzadah spoke the words into his compact sat phone, almost wincing at the sour taste they left inside his mouth.

"But *do* you?" asked Ehsan Abarkhyl, his immediate commander in the field. "Captain Qayoumi wants results. We *both* do. And we want them now!"

"Yes, sir. But in the dark—"

"We all know that the nights are dark," Abarkhyl cut him off. "And now the sun has risen, yes?"

"Yes, but—"

"Your Red Unit is trained to fight by day or night, is that not true? You are accustomed to this, surely?"

For a fraction of a second, Omar flashed back to the last American movie he'd seen, some mindless farce about an airliner, where one idiot actor warns another, "Don't call me Shirley!" Jamalzadah felt a deranged impulse to giggle, but he stifled it before it got him killed.

And said, "Yes, sir. They are. *We* are."

"Well, then...?"

"We dispatched the drones as ordered, sir. They are equipped with thermographic cameras, and—"

"FLIR," Abarkhyl interrupted him again. "I'm well aware of forward-looking infrared technology, Omar."

"Yes, sir. Of course, sir."

"And? What of it?"

"Nothing, I'm afraid, sir."

"How can there be *nothing*, Omar? Are you telling me you've lost the spy? That he's become invisible? A ghost, perhaps?"

"No, sir. But FLIR requires a contact, body heat presumably. And if the subject has concealed himself, shielded from recognition by a drone circling above the desert floor..."

"All right, enough. If the technology has failed us, what about your *eyes*, Omar? Can you not see them crossing open desert, standing out like a darkling beetle on a dinner plate?"

"Sir, we believe they travel only after nightfall."

"When your drones should spot them, yes?"

"Unless they have some means of masking body temperature, sir."

"Such as...?"

"Thermal camouflage that may deflect and scatter energy from the environment, sir. I'm told Crusaders call them 'turkey suits', after the foil wrapping placed over barnyard fowl while they are baking in an oven."

"Turkey suits. You wish me to tell Captain Qayoumi that you've failed at your assignment due to one man putting on a so-called turkey suit?"

"No, sir! But if the drones are ineffective, then it may require more men and vehicles to cover an extended area."

"You shall make do with what you have, Omar, and we expect a speedy resolution to this problem. Is that clear? You understand me?"

"Yes, sir."

"I hope so. Because failure in this case is not an option. Failure in this case, Omar, means that you wind up on the cross."

CHAPTER 7

Kunduz Province, Afghanistan

They left the mine shaft after sundown and resumed their trek northward, crossing into southern Kunduz Province some two hours later.

Named after its most significant geographic feature—the Kunduz River, an irregularly flowing tributary of the Amu Darya that serves as the Afghan border with Uzbekistan—Kunduz Province spans 3,100 square miles and claims a population of some 954,000 people drawn from nine different, sometimes hostile ethnic groups.

For many province residents, life has deteriorated since the U.S. invasion. In Kunduz, where 25 percent of family homes had access to clean drinking water in 2005, the figure declined to 11 percent six years later. School enrollment dropped by 12 percent during those years, with one in five province residents deemed illiterate. Subsistence agriculture is the primary pursuit. The only contact with outsiders not in military uniforms is Shērkhān Bandar, a dry port wedged between the province and Tajikistan.

Sara Durell wanted no part of Shērkhān Bandar or Tajikistan. The last-ditch course she'd plotted led them toward Uzbekistan, a tremulous, inconstant ally of America, but still the best around, unless you caught a flight to Ankara, 1,920-odd miles to the west.

And with Jack Cody at her side, there was a fighting chance that she would make it after all.

They walked in silence for the most part, ears pricked for the humming sound of drones somewhere above them in the desert's star-speckled night, watching for headlights that would mark a motorized patrol. That might turn out to be the Taliban or the Afghan National Army, maybe even an American scouring party, though Sara doubted the latter. Western troops, from what one U.S. President once called the "coalition of the willing", tried to spend their nights in bivouac, behind barbed wire, unless some compelling emergency drew them off into the perilous boondocks.

Sufficient evil stalked the Afghan landscape during broad daylight without stumbling across dope caravans and spoiling any faction's profit-sharing scheme.

But now, damn it, Sara couldn't ignore the headlights glaring up ahead, a mile or so in front of them, directly in their path. It looked like half a dozen vehicles to her, and Cody spotted them at the same time.

"Well, shit!" he told the desert night.

It would take time to loop around the obstacle to east or west, adding at least an hour to their nightly travel time, hoping the whole way that whoever occupied those vehicles stayed put instead of fanning out to sweep the open countryside.

"Some kind of village up there, right?" Jack asked.

He must have known the answer before speaking. Sara didn't have to guess, after she'd memorized the maps available from Langley at the outset of her mission. And she knew that Jack, despite short notice, would have done the same.

She answered anyway. "It is. I couldn't tell you what it's called, though."

"Taliban supporters?"

Sara shrugged, then realized he wasn't watching her, eyes focused from a distance on that bright spot in the night. "Who knows, out here? It could go either way."

"They're not afraid of letting people know they're here."

"So, sympathizers, then," she said, playing the odds.

"Or not. A hunt's on, right?"

For me, she thought. And said, "No doubt."

"And maybe Afghan regulars are in on it, after last night's fireworks."

"I wouldn't be surprised."

"Whoever drove out here, they're likely wanting answers."

"So?"

Jack glanced at her across one shoulder. "So, the smart thing is to go around and let them be. It slows us down a bit, but if we stop..."

"I hear you. Let's get started, then."

A gunshot punctuated Sara's comment. There was no mistaking the echo of a Kalashnikov's report. No modern soldier worth his or her salt could possibly mistake it, even if the caliber was hard to guess. Hell, you could even download AK sound effects these days onto your laptop or make it the ring tone for your cell phone.

Crazy times.

"Somebody didn't answer quick enough, I guess," Jack said.

"Remember *Chinatown*?" she asked him.

"Polanski and Nicholson's nose," Cody replied.

"No, I was thinking of the end. 'Forget it Jake, it's China-town'."

"And like I said, we need to move."

Sara nodded, then caught herself. "No, wait, goddammit."

"What?"

"I need to see what's happening," she said, and started moving toward the distant lights.

Omar Jamalzadah believed in leading by example., asking nothing of his men that he was not prepared to do himself.

Just now he stood over an old man's twitching corpse, breathing the cordite smell from his AK-74, ignoring the hole its 5.45mm slug had drilled into the victim's wrinkled face.

Captain Isani of the ISI had told Omar that CIA headquarters paid five thousand U.S. dollars for the first AK-74 captured by *mujahideen* during the 1980s Afghan-Russian war.

It might be true, Jamalzadah. Crusaders had no end of cash to burn on trivialities worldwide. Five thousand would be nothing next to what they'd spent arming Muslim guerillas Ronald Reagan viewed as freedom fighters.

Was it not poetic justice that those same jihadists later turned and bit the manicured hand that fed them table scraps?

Omar waited until a measure of the village women's wailing had subsided, then shouted over their heads, "All right, who's next? I've told you what we need, and if you can't supply the information, why should any of you live to see another sunrise? Quickly, now! Who knows where we can find the damned Crusader fugitive?"

A man spoke up from the front row of hastily assembled villagers, cheeks glistening with most unmanly tears. "Sir," he replied, "we have already told you that we've seen no strangers here, much less Americans."

"You've told me that, it's true," Jamalzadah agreed. "And I call you a lying heap of camel dung."

Before the angry murmuring of other villagers could gather steam, Omar reminded them, "The infiltrator—no, the *murderer*—we seek is moving northward. This hog wallow that you call a village lies along his route of march. Even Crusader scum cannot survive the desert without water, he? Unless you all have sacrificed your brains to opium or hashish, *someone* must have seen him. *Someone* must know *something*."

Standing almost near enough to touch, much less to kill, the villager who'd spoken up tried to continue. "Sir—"

Jamalzadah spoke over him. "Enough! Unless you plan to

speak the truth, be man enough to kneel and join your village elder on his way to *Jahannam*." Using the Muslim term for Hell.

The villager stared back at him, then slowly knelt before Omar. It wasn't what the Taliban Red Unit leader had expected, but he shrugged as if it made no difference.

"Your choice, then. And whoever's next in line to die, consider this pathetic fool's example. "Hamid! Step forward!"

Hamid Munadi, sergeant of the unit, instantly stepped up to Omar's side. "Yes, sir!" he snapped.

"This one is yours, Sergeant. We shall take turns killing the rest until one of them speaks."

Hamid shouldered his AK-107, sighting down its barrel, aiming at the trembling fellow on his knees. Jamalzadah waited to hear the shot, but when it came, the villager did not collapse.

Instead, the shot came from somewhere behind Omar, striking its target with a wet slap that sprayed fresh, warm blood across the left side of his face and neck.

Jack Cody knew that intervening to prevent another execution was a bad idea. The worst, in fact. Off hand, he couldn't think of anything more foolish than to pick a fight with Taliban guerillas in the midst of their attempt to flee Afghanistan, risking their lives for strangers who most likely hated all Americans and thereby risking not only discovery by their opponents, but inviting death—or worse, capture while still alive.

He knew all that but didn't waste his breath trying to stop Sara Durell. He knew her, too, and realized his words would fall on deaf ears if he sought to reason with her in the face of cold-blooded murder.

As if they didn't deal in extralegal death each day, year-round.

So, he'd argued first against approaching, then against lending a hand, but when Sara hoisted the AKS-74U to her shoulder, aiming with the stubby carbine's adjustable iron sights, there was nothing to be done except for Jack to back her play, however ill-conceived it seemed to him.

Her first shot was on target, as expected, taking down the designated hitter, splattering the guy beside him who'd been giving orders with a steamy bath of gore. The man in charge was still recoiling from that bloody slap across the face when Cody brought his AK-107 into action, triggering a three-round burst that nailed a pair of Taliban guerillas stationed by one of the raiding party's trucks, a Tata Motors SK1613 4.5-ton rig indistinguishable from those used by units of the Afghan National Army.

The two went down together, thrashing, their demise reducing the strike force by roughly one-tenth. The goons still breathing tried to duck and cover behind other vehicles, including an M113 armored personnel carrier, an M1117 Armored Security Vehicle, a couple of Ford Ranger light tactical vehicles, and a Toyota Hilux four-door pickup truck. The M113 mounted an M2 .50-caliber machine gun, while the M1117 boasted the Russian equivalent, an NSVT 12.7mm coaxial machine gun.

Each of those man-shredders was being handled, at that moment, by a turbaned, bearded triggerman, with backup to replace the ammo belts their guns consumed.

While Sara fired and fired again into the scattering jihadi ranks, Jack swung his weapon toward the M113 APC and fired a 40mm HE round from its GP-25 *Kostyor* grenade launcher. His projectile struck the APC's turret, two feet or less in front of the machine-gunner. Forget about the sixty-five-foot lethal radius. You might as well have shoved the gunner and his pal into a woodchipper.

And after that, it all went straight to Hell.

Sara ducked and flinched when Jack's grenade exploded to her left, against one of the APCs. She heard screams as the shrapnel from that blast stung members of the raiding party and the Talibs started scattering like roaches when the kitchen lights come on.

Cody had taken out one of the heavy machine guns, but now its mate, mounted atop the M1117, was rattling and roaring in the night, green tracers mixed in with the FMJ rounds it was spraying up and down the foremost row of village shanties, punching holes through plywood walls and peeling back whatever passed for roofing on those meager homes.

She tried to spot the shot-caller who'd been directing executions, but the prick had mingled with his erstwhile victims, keeping his head down and seeking any cover he could find in no-man's land, no doubt praying to Allah for protection from the firestorm he had started.

Rather than stand idle, waiting for her shot, Sara moved out in the direction of the M1117. Her first stop was beside the M113, badly damaged now, its turret smoking and blood-stained, but probably still capable of being driven from the scene. First thing, though, someone had to get behind its steering wheel, and she was bent on seeing that nobody did.

The terrorists were in a panic, trying to discover who had brought them under fire and failing for the most part. Some had started firing randomly into the ranks of fleeing villagers and their pathetic hovels, others turned Kalashnikovs against the outer darkness as if shadows could be slain. The squad's surviving 12.7mm gun was spraying tracers in an arc that cut through men, women and children, taking down at least one of the shooter's comrades in the process.

Madness.

Sara pushed up from her crouch beside the M113, aimed across its damaged hood, her carbine's sights framing the other APC's machine-gunner in profile, swiveling his NSVT with one hand clutching its pistol grip, the other braced on its side-mounted ammo box.

Her first 5.54mm round sliced through his neck like an icepick piercing cheese, knocking him sideways while his weapon tilted skyward, firing at the stars above. Her second shot drilled him through center mass and dropped him, even as his sidekick stepped up to resume the MG's bloody work.

Sara shot him next, one slug all it took to put him down

inside the APC's turret, and then she sent one more slug to deactivate the NSVT's firing mechanism, taking it out of the fight for good. A gunsmith could repair it, but just now they were in short supply.

She had withdrawn a step, was starting on a second, when a bullet struck the M113's how and ricocheted, spraying her face and neck with chips of paint. Cursing, she took a quick look for the shooter, thought she might have glimpsed him, but a stream of running villagers was sweeping past him, so she held her fire and didn't reach for one of her Russian F1 frag grenades.

The Taliban had killed or wounded plenty of the shabby little town's inhabitants already, without Sara's help.

But had she helped at all, or only made things worse?

That was a straight-up judgment call, but instinct told her that the Talibs would have kept on killing until someone spilled their knowledge of her whereabouts—which none of them possessed. Unchecked, the massacre would certainly have laid waste to the settlement. This way, at least, there was a chance some of its people might survive.

And then go...where?

That's not my problem, Sara told herself, and got back to the war at hand.

Jack Cody was about to hit the second Taliban APC with another 40mm round when Sara beat him to it, taking down the turret gunner and his backup man. Neither of the Red Unit's armored vehicles had drivers in their cabs, which left them both immobilized for now.

If he could keep them that way till his other adversaries were eliminated, Cody thought the M1117 might help them make some faster mileage toward the Uzbek border, maybe even traveling by daylight until someone spotted them, perhaps using one of the Boeing Insitu ScanEagle drones first marketed some sixteen years ago, adopted by the Afghan National Army around 2005.

Smart money said that if the ANA had some new plaything, then their adversaries likely had it too, and were employing it to raise hell with their enemies in power. In fact, he guessed it was a ScanEagle he'd heard buzzing above the desert yesterday. Given their present circumstance, whichever side had sent the flying eye aloft would be irrelevant.

Right now, Jack still had well-armed enemies to kill.

He started spotting Talibs, firing single rounds or short bursts from his AK-107 as the moving targets might require. Once he had put slugs in flight, he couldn't guarantee a clean kill, couldn't even swear a bullet might not drill his chosen target through-and-through before it brought down someone else, but that was war.

You played the cards that Fate had dealt you, then you lived with the result—assuming that you lived at all.

And if you lost...so, what? The choices offered by the planet's great philosophers were either some nebulous afterlife or just oblivion. Since Jack had lost his family, he'd had no doubt which one he'd pick, given a choice.

A Talib broke out of the crowd and tried to reach the M1117, running hunched over like a quarterback, hugging an AK-407 rather than a football. Cody tracked him for a few yards, hearing bullets whisper overhead but standing firm, until the runner reached his goal and tried to scramble up the left side of the APC.

A second later, he appeared over the top, hauling himself into the armored vehicle's turret, but he forgot to duck down out of sight immediately. He was grappling with the NSVT mounted there when Cody shot him in the face from thirty yards.

It was a quick kill, although not exactly clean. Most weren't, in Jack's experience, since dying humans have a tendency to leak like flimsy plastic shopping bags when they expire. Even when strangled, bludgeoned, or whatever, once the muscles had relaxed in death, you had a wet mess on your hands.

Good news for CSI types trying to collect forensic evidence, perhaps, but for a killer bent on covering his tracks it was another story.

Rather than allow the next jihadist and the next to make a run for the unmanned heavy machine gun, Jack decided he should claim it for himself. Breaking for cover, he approached the APC in time to meet another Talib circling around to board the vehicle through its backdoor and find at least some measure of security behind its Modular Expandable Armor System, or maybe fire it up and try to get the hell away from here.

Too late.

Jack shot him twice and left him cooling in the sand, then ducked into the vehicle himself and scrambled forward to the turret, interrupted by the task of dragging corpses clear before he hunched behind the 12.7mm gun.

Its ammo belts were chintzy, not the best design in Jack's professional opinion. Each belt held only fifty rounds, expended at an average rate of 750 rounds per minute on full-auto fire. In combat, that meant burning through a belt every four seconds, stopping to reload, while the American M2 used belts of rounds, while the heavy-barrel M2HB model featured a selection mechanism that allowed for single shots to variable rates on either side of forty rounds per minute—better both for accuracy and forestalling burnout of the weapon's barrel.

Screw that.

Cody clutched the fifty-five pound gun and rattled off whatever still remained of its old belt, firing well over turbaned heads to spare the innocent, then grabbed another ammo box—twenty-four pounds right there—and managed to reload it in a rush before the first Talibs wised up and started firing rifle shots his way.

The trick, now, was to finish off his enemies with Sara's help, and without killing any of the village's panicked inhabitants.

With luck and skill, Jack thought he just might pull it off.

Omar Jamalzadah fumbled the sat phone in his haste and

dropped it on the ground, stooped to retrieve it just as some-one cut loose with the heavy Russian NSVT from M1117 tactical vehicle. The storm of bullets hurtling overhead forced Omar belly-down on desert sand, but now he had the phone in hand, punching the numbers that should put him through to Ehsan Abarkhyl at province headquarters.

A bullet struck the ground within six inches of his face, flinging grit into Omar's left eye.

"*Mur kwas!*" he swore in Pashto. "*Hanzeer bacha!*"

Wriggling backward, Omar tried to clear his burning eye by swiping at it with one hand, but only seemed to make it worse, more painful. Crawling like a lizard, pushing with his boots and elbows, he was halfway to the cover of a peasant's hovel when another hot round found him, grazed his shoulder, sending him into a fetal curl.

Weeping with pain now, Omar cleared the last few yards after the creeping manner of a wounded reptile, reached the hut that was his destination, and struggled to stand erect in its doorway. The sat phone started ringing in his hand, as his call was connected.

Finally!

Omar had no hope of relief from headquarters, but duty bound him to report their contact with an enemy, whoever that might be. He had no hope of rescue, even thought that might be worse if it could be accomplished, placing him at Sediq Qayoumi's mercy after failing in his quest.

Would it be crucifixion, then? Perhaps beheading? Or would Sediq simply have him shot down by a firing squad?

No matter. Omar knew he must report, in any case.

"*Khe chare?*" Omar recognized the voice of Ehsan Abarkhyl, asking him, "*Da tsok dai?*"

"It's me," Omar replied.

"Where are you? Is that gunfire? What is happening?"

Jamalzadah was on the verge of answering, prepared to plead his hopeless case, when suddenly he felt the impact of a hammer stroke against his lower back. He gasped in agony, clutching his stomach where the bullet's exit wound was pumping bright, warm blood, and crumpled to the to the ground, keeping his death grip on the telephone.

Sara Durell pried lifeless fingers from their grip on the sat phone. The Talib she had gunned down gave it up reluctantly, as if some part of him still felt responsible for keeping the device from hostile hands.

A futile effort, even if she had to snap one of his fingers over backwards with an ugly *crack*.

Rising, she held the sat phone to her ear and heard a male, authoritative voice demanding, "*Khe chare? D tsok dai?*"

More Pashto gibberish she couldn't translate followed that, while Sara listened without speaking. Seconds passed, the fellow at the other end of their connection ramping up his agitation when no answer was forthcoming. Finally, he shouted something that she took to be a threat, and Sara figured she should let him off the hook—or give a tug and sink it deeper, as the case might be.

"Your boys are dead, asshole," she said. "If I have anything to say about it, you'll be next."

And then she cut the link, dropped the sat phone, and trod it underfoot until its electronic guts spilled free. The man whose name she didn't know might still have some way to discover where it was, maybe a built-in GPS device she hadn't managed to destroy, and that was fine. Before a squad of reinforcements reached the village, she and Jack should be long gone.

As if her thought had conjured him, Cody spoke to her now from close at hand.

"All done?"

"I am," she said. "No Talibs left?"

"None breathing," he confirmed. "The other natives may be getting restless, though."

Jack had a point. A couple dozen villagers, unwounded, had returned to eye them from a distance, none with weapons yet, though some were glaring at the two Americans—what they might think of as "Crusaders"—with a bit less gratitude than Sara thought appropriate.

"We need to book," she said.

"No sweat," Cody replied. "We've three rides to choose from, not counting the armored cars."

She scanned the pickup trucks, two Fords and one Toyota. None of them had any damage she could spot, off hand.

"You worried about being LoJacked?" she asked Cody.

"Doubtful. Government hackers could break into the system and use it against them. No real way to guard against that kind of thing with Taliban technology."

"So, what? We drive it till we're out of gas, then ditch it?"

"Works for me," Jack said. "On top of which, the pickups all have jerrycans of backup fuel on board. With any luck, if we can find someplace to hide it during daylight hours, we could make it to the border by tomorrow night."

She thought about it for another second before nodding. Said, "Why not."

They weren't exactly overwhelmed with options now, and if Plan B fell through, what did they have to lose?

Nothing except their lives.

CHAPTER 8

Kunduz Province

"You ever hear that song, 'I Drove All Night'?" Sara inquired. "Celine Dione?"

"I have," Jack said, "but I preferred the first recording."

"Cyndi Lauper?"

"Nope. Roy Orbison did it the year before he died, but it wasn't released till after Lauper's version went Top Ten."

"Jeez, is there anything you *don't* know?" Sara asked.

"A little bit. I *do* know Jason Priestly did the Orbison video, with Jennifer Connelly."

"*Any*way, this jaunt just brought it back to mind. Seems like forever since I've heard it."

"You could check the radio," Cody replied, "but you'll most likely get Aryana Sayeed singing 'Gule Sib'."

"Enough, already. Driving through the desert here just made me think of it, that's all."

"Okay. One thing I *don't* know," Jack said, "is your plan for crossing at the border, if we get that far."

"I'll need to call about that, since Plan A crapped out."

"Check in with Washington?"

"The DI first," she said, meaning Director of Central Intelligence at Langley. "After that, with Boyd."

"That guy. You ever wonder what he's really thinking when you ask him something?"

"All the time. Hey, that's the life we chose, right?"

"Some of us," Jack said.

"Yourself included?"

"Sure, why not?" he granted. "Some might say I got dragged into it, but when you boil it down, I did it to myself."

"Jack—"

"No, I'm serious."

"You were deployed, remember? And you aren't a psychic, last I heard. You couldn't know something would happen on the home front while you were away."

"It was my job to know, Sara. I took a vow."

"And took an oath, as well, the same as I did. You were under orders, serving in the line of duty."

No point in reminding Jack that it had cost him everything he loved. She knew a waking hour didn't pass without that preying on his mind, nor would he find escape from it in dreams.

"Whatever," he responded, a dismissive tone. "About Plan B…"

"Long story short, we have to get across the Friendship Bridge."

"Uh-huh. Sounds like you left most of the story out."

"Because it isn't written yet."

Officially, the so-called Friendship Bridge between Hyraton, Afghanistan, and Termez in Uzbekistan was the only way across the Amu Darya borderline—that is, without a battery of guns blazing away. The bridge had started as a Central Asian Railway crossing in the early 1900s, nearly three kilometers in length, improved and strengthened by successive teams of engineers over a century and more, closed by the Taliban during the 1990s, reopened during 2001. Its main function today was freight traffic and haulage, but Durell knew there were ways to circumvent that hiccup with the help of well-placed friends.

The question, now, was whether anyone back home would help her cross with Jack.

Dawn's pallid light was breaking to the east, the onset of her fourth day in Afghanistan. Three days too long, that was, with no end yet in sight.

"We'd better find a place to stash this ride," Jack said. "Eyes peeled."

"I'm watching," she assured him.

Two miles farther north, they came upon a small and seemingly abandoned farm. There was no sign of its former inhabitants as they approached in the Toyota pickup, circling once around the house and what she took for a small barn of sorts. When they got out, guns ready, Jack scouted the house, while Sara checked the outbuilding and found it vacant, save for desert long-eared bats rustling around the sagging rafters.

Nothing there to fear unless she climbed aloft and started grabbing them, the very last thing on her mind right now.

The first was shelter from the rising sun.

Second was calling home.

And third was sleep.

She stepped outside, saw Jack returning from the empty house, and waved for him to hide the pickup in, concealed from flying eyes. When that was done, the warped doors closed as far as they could go, she turned to face him.

"I'll get on the horn and keep it short," she said. "Then breakfast, and some rest?"

"Suits me," Jack said. He rummaged in a cargo pocket, brought out an afghani coin, and said, "A flip for first watch suit you?"

Bamyan Province

ISI Captain Mohammed Isani lit a Mareb cigarette from Yemen, drew the acrid smoke into his lungs, and blew it back across his desk into Sediq Qayoumi's face. The Talib officer made no complaint, despite the latest *fatwah* against smoking issued by Islamic scholars citing health concerns, exceeding— as Isani thought—orders contained within the great Quran.

When he supposed Sediq had squirmed and sweated long enough, Isani said, "So, tell me how you came to lose a strike force of so-called elite soldiers."

"There is a village in Kunduz Province..."

"I've been advised of the geography," Isani interrupted. "Now answer my question."

Qayoumi shifted in his straight-backed wooden chair, designed for maximum discomfort. "It appears that they were ambushed while interrogating peasant villagers about the fugitive we seek."

"'Appears'? Is there some doubt? You think, perhaps, it was some sort of murder-suicide?"

"No, sir. They *were* ambushed. As to precisely how it happened, how so many men were taken by surprise and overcome...I cannot say as yet."

"I trust you have inquired, Sediq? Questioned these peasants you referred to?"

"The village was abandoned when our reinforcements reached it. We are searching for survivors."

"Disappeared, you say? Have they evaporated into thin air, then? Perhaps they were abducted by a flying saucer?"

Sediq Qayoumi pulled a sour face. "Hardly," he said. "They left tracks which are being followed, but once they escaped into the nearby mountains..."

"Now you seek not only one Crusader who first spied upon your headquarters, and now has massacred your troops, but also fleeing villagers? To what end, may I ask?"

"For information," Sediq answered. "No doubt you recall demanding it."

"And now I note your failure to deliver. What am I to do with you, Sediq?"

The Talib stiffened, gripped the hard arms of his chair,

leaned slightly forward. "Nothing, Captain. But you might strive to recall that you are in Afghanistan, on foreign soil, not in Islamabad."

Isani smiled at that. "Of course, Sediq. You are correct. Why should I offer you advice or counsel in this matter? Doubtless you'll resolve it without any help from me or from my agency. You have no further need of money or materiel assistance either, I presume."

To that, no answer was forthcoming. But if looks could kill, Isani would have been a dead man where he sat, behind his desk.

"Well?" Isani prodded his unhappy guest.

Stiffly, reluctantly, Sediq replied, "There is one thing."

"Which is...?"

"My second in command, Ehsan Abarkhyl, you have met him."

"Spit it out, Sediq."

"During the village skirmish, as it ended, he received a call from one of our satellite phones."

"Go on."

"The phone belonged to Omar Jamalzadah, leader of the Red Unit involved."

"And?"

"Omar did not speak when Ehsan answered, but Ehsan tells me someone else did speak. It seemed to be a woman's voice."

Isani felt his scalp tingling as he ground out his cigarette in a cheap metal ashtray. "And what did she say?"

"According to Ehsan, she said, 'Your boys are dead, asshole. If I have anything to say about it, you'll be next.' He took pains to recall her words precisely."

"So. As I thought, a female agent, then."

"I can't believe she wiped out all our men, acting alone. From evidence recovered at the scene, there were at least two persons firing."

"Two against...how many was it?"

"Thirty-eight," Qayoumi said.

"It seems you have your work cut out for you, Sediq. May I expect good news sometime today?"

"No doubt, sir."

"Then I leave you to it. Waste no further time correcting your mistakes."

Washington, D.C.

The sat phone's muted sound demanded Denham Boyd's attention. As he answered it, he could already feel his stomach clenching.

"Go," he said.

Sara Durell's familiar voice reached him from halfway round the planet. Boyd tried to imagine how she'd looked the last time they spoke face to face, at Langley, and was troubled when it wouldn't come to him at once.

"Still kicking," she informed him, "just in case you're hearing something to the contrary."

"Too bad about those other guys," Boyd said, keeping it terse despite the scrambler program and cutout relays.

"They did their best," Sara replied.

"Not good enough, I guess. You missed the party?"

"Nope. In fact, I had a ringside seat."

Boyd blinked at that. Answered, "Yet, here you are."

"I had some help I wasn't counting on," she said.

Now Denham's stomach gave a lazy barrel roll. "That other guy?" he asked.

"The very same. Lucky for me, I'd say."

"You ought to know, I told him to stay out of it."

"Same thing I would've done," she answered, "if the shoe was on the other foot."

"Okay, then. No hard feelings?"

"I'm not looking backwards," she replied. "But we could use some help down range."

"Just tell me where and when," Boyd said.

"Not yet. We're working on it, though."

"I won't ask where you are right now."

"Best not to," she agreed. "I need to tell you something, though."

"I'm listening."

"There was another incident last night."

"How'd that come up?" Boyd asked, avoiding the specifics.

"We walked in on something and decided that it shouldn't happen. Just in case you start to hear some rumbles."

"Thanks for the heads-up."

"About the other thing…"

"Go on."

"Best keep your phone handy, regardless of the time."

"Will do. I'll pass the word upstairs, such as it is."

"Figured you would. Don't want the royal bowels in an uproar."

"I'm not even touching that," Boyd said.

"And I don't blame you. Later."

Boyd was working on "goodbye" when he was cut off by a wispy, long-range dial tone and the link shut down. He mouthed a silent curse and stashed the sat phone back where it belonged, in his desk drawer. Out of sight, but very seldom out of mind.

And now, he had to face the president again.

As Denham Boyd reached for the desktop intercom, to reach his P.A., he was hoping that the Big Man's schedule would keep him busy for a while, distracted from the life-or-death events unfolding in Afghanistan.

Kunduz Province

Jack Cody didn't like to eavesdrop on a friend, but Sara kept her call to Washington cryptic and short, nothing to jeopardize security in any case. When she was done talking to Denham Boyd on Pennsylvania Avenue, she drifted back to where Jack rested in their stolen pickup's corrugated bed.

"All done, for now," she said.

"No border-crossing plans?"

"It's premature for that."

In case they didn't make it, Jack presumed. Why mobilize resources for the dead and gone?

"You want to get some sleep, there's ample time. Driving all night, and so on."

"Not right now. I'm feeling wired, you know?"

"Been there."

"But not right now?"

He shrugged. "Not sleepy yet."

"You need your rest, though."

"Like you said, we've got all day."

"But I was thinking," Sara went on. "Maybe we could rest... together, for a while."

He tried a smile but wasn't sure it worked. "Last time before the war? Like that?"

"Too late," she said. "We're in the war already."

"So, more like a furlough, then?"

She answered with a question of her own. "What do you think?"

Jack got the smile right this time, as he answered back, "I think you might be onto something, there."

Her smile reflected Jack's. "I don't suppose they left a blanket in his heap?"

"No sign of one. It has a backseat, though."

"Like high school? Going to the drive-in movie?"

"They were history when I was coming up," he said.

"Me, too. We had an old one, though, abandoned, two or three miles out of town. Sometimes the kids would go out there and…well, you know."

"I'm trying to imagine it," he said.

Her fingers found the buttons of her desert camo shirt, starting to open them. "It hasn't been *that* long…has it?"

"It's feeling longer by the second."

"Ouch!"

"I haven't touched you yet."

Third button from the top was open now, her slim hands working on the fourth. Jack liked the view but thought a leer might be over the top. She stopped there, watching him, and said, "You want to help me out here, mister?"

"I believe you're doing fine."

The shirt came off and landed in a small heap, carelessly. The sports bra Sara wore beneath it wasn't camouflaged and wasn't leaving much to Jack's imagination.

"The backseat, you said?"

"First thing that came to me," Cody replied.

"So, are you coming?"

Sara trailed her fingertips across his lap as she slid past him, landing on her feet behind the pickup's tailgate.

"I might," Jack answered, "if you keep that up."

"Don't try passing the buck," she said. "Keeping it up is your job."

"I'll do my best."

"I'm counting on it."

She'd kicked her boots off and was stepping out of her DCU trousers by the time Jack got his shirt off, sports bra dropped beside the pants and footwear. Sara had the backdoor on the pickup driver's side open before she paused and spoke again.

"Oh, wait," she said. "We need protection."

"What? With all this hardware?"

"Jack, I'm serious."

"No worries," he replied. "Seems like they pack the damnedest things with MREs."

Baghlan Province

"I hate him!" said Sediq Qayoumi, fairly spitting out the words. "He speaks to me as if this were his country, rather than our own."

"I've never trusted Pakistanis," Ehsan Abarkhyl replied. "And yet..."

"We still need their support," Sediq acknowledged.

"Until we have claimed the victory," Abarkhyl said. "Then we can sweep them all away."

"A day worth looking forward to."

"But in the meantime, sir..."

"You're right. We must locate and punish those responsible for murdering our men."

Qayoumi knew the only fitting punishment for that was slow, torturous death, but first they had to find the woman who'd made fools of them so far, along with any others who were aiding her.

"What do our soldiers searching at the village say?" he

asked Ehsan.

"One of the first team's vehicles was taken, sir," Abarkhyl said. "They don't know yet who was responsible or where it's gone."

"*Spie zoe!*" Omar swore. "Can they not follow tracks across the desert?"

"A dust storm started just as they arrived. They are comparing it to a scirocco."

"Idiots! Why would one of the village peasants steal a vehicle? Where would they go, if it were true? There's no one in that stretch of godforsaken waste to buy it from them, is there?"

"Doubtful, sir. But without tracks—"

"Yes, yes, I know. The search must focus northward now. Forget about the villagers, wherever they may be. You heard a woman's voice over the telephone, Ehsan. I had to say it, but that *sada kway* Isani was correct for once. It should be easy to detect a woman—an *American* woman, at that—crossing the province in a stolen pickup truck."

"In theory, at least."

"To hell with theory, Ehsan! We must get results before we lose this *kus* into Uzbekistan."

"The destination is determined, then?" asked Abarkhyl.

"Simplicity itself," Omar replied. "Where else might a Crusader and a lowly woman go for refuge in the region? Not Pakistan and not Iran. Her only allies to be found—and not strong ones, at that—are the Uzbeks."

"With any luck, we can get there ahead of her," said Ehsan. "And if need be, we can even stop her on the Friendship Bridge itself."

"A long-range sniper?" Omar mused.

Ehsan nodded. "Red Units, as you know, have Dragunov rifles taken from Russians in the war preceding this one, sir. With a PSO-1 telescopic sight, skilled marksmen can drop targets from a half-mile, sometimes farther."

"That might provoke an incident," Sediq cautioned.

"Perhaps, sir. But who really cares what Uzbeks think? Let them complain to Kabul or to the United Nations, if they dare. Once it is known they operate with spies and terrorists from the United States, they may regret poking a stick into the anthill."

"So be it, then. But if they have a chance to stop this *loor* short of the border, they must take it."

"Understood, sir."

"Capture her alive, if possible, for questioning. If that should prove too difficult, bring back her head and post the video worldwide."

"It shall be done."

"You should go north yourself, Ehsan. Take charge of the Red Unit. Prod them toward success."

A heartbeat's hesitation, followed by, "My pleasure, sir."

"And should you fail…"

"Yes, sir."

"Do not come back alive."

Kunduz Province

Sara Durell lay limp and spent in Cody's arms. Her heavy breathing—almost panting—in the midst of it had finally subsided to an easy, measured pace. When she glanced up at Jack, she saw his eyes were closed.

"Are you awake?" she asked, half whispering.

"Oh, yeah. Relaxed, though, for the first time in I don't know how long."

"Nothing like a little R and R," she granted.

"I'm not sure I'd call what we just did 'a little'."

Sara had to laugh at that, but softly, in appreciation of the sentiment. "I guess I wouldn't either," she agreed.

"Could make things harder, though," Jack said.

She reached for him. "Again? So soon?"

"Not that," he said, but placed his hand over her own, not pushing it away. "I'm thinking more about tonight."

"Oh? What about it?"

"When the Taliban finds us or we run into them," Jack said. "It could get sticky."

"Want to spell that out?" she asked.

He thought about it for a moment, then pressed on. "Before, when we were fighting in the village, it was all about survival."

"So?"

"So, put a new twist on it and it gets more…complicated."

"Whoa, boy. I can see where this is going."

"Break that down for me."

"I feel your inner caveman kicking in."

"Say what?"

"Don't even try denying it, okay?"

"I don't—"

"You were about to say that your efficiency's been compromised. You can't go into battle with the same swashbuckling attitude now that you feel bound to protect me. Am I right?"

"Well..."

"Don't even go there, Jack. I made it through firefights before we ever met. As far as this gig goes, all right, I lost a partner it started going downhill after that, but if you hadn't dropped in from the blue—"

"Go on. Say it."

"I was watching when the SEALs went down. I'd call it sixty-forty that I could have slipped away from that without a helping hand."

"So? I was in the neighborhood."

"One hell of a commute."

He shrugged. "I get around. There's no denying it."

"And that won't change. We're not a couple, Jack. Just two ships passing in the night."

"Ships of the desert," Cody cracked.

"Smartass."

"I'm known for that, too."

"No one could deny it."

"So, what are you saying, Sara?"

"We get through this, any way we can, and things go back to normal. That okay by you?"

"Sounds fair. You don't mind if I think about it sometimes, though?"

"I might be disappointed if you didn't."

"Hey, I aim to please."

"And hit the mark. I'll give you that."

"So, no regrets?"

"Not one. On my end, anyway."

"Nor me. But I was thinking?"

"What?"

"We've still got six or seven hours left before the sun goes down and we can blow this pop stand."

"And?"

"I'd just like to see if I can make another bullseye."

"It's a damned good thing you didn't say a hole-in-one."

"You sound surprised. Somebody tell you I'm not sensitive to nuance?"

Her hand went back to work as Sara said, "Shut up, will you? We're wasting time."

The White House

Denham Boyd had called ahead to make sure that the president was free and got the green light to stop by, ten minutes tops. He figured it should only take half of that time, unless The Man lapsed into one of his world-famous talking jags and slowed things down.

As Boyd entered the Oval Office, for a split-second he

thought he was alone, but then a toilet flushed in the executive wash, followed by the muffled droning of a hot-air drier likely wall-mounted beside the sink. Boyd couldn't say for sure, since he had never been beyond the restroom door, but where else would it be?

"So, what's the word?" the president inquired, without preamble.

"They're still in transit, Mister President."

"They?"

"Yes, sir. When the SEALs went down, we had another operative in the neighborhood. He's headed for the border with our asset."

"Where are they at this moment?"

Denham swallowed hard and bit the bullet. "Difficult to say, sir."

"Difficult to say? I understood you tracked these kinds of operations via satellite, by GPS."

"Normally yes, sir."

"Stop the tap dance, Boyd, and I mean now! I've spent my life in politics, and I can smell a bunch of weasel words ten miles away. When you say 'normally', that tells me something's badly out of whack."

"It seems they have disabled their transponders, sir."

"Deliberately?"

"That's unknown at present. Battlefield conditions may have been responsible, or—"

"Specify the 'battlefield conditions' for me, Boyd. I know about the SEALs. That's being handled through Naval Intelligence. Have these two agents been involved in fighting someone else, since SEAL Team X went dark?"

"There was an incident. An isolated village, Mister President. Apparently—"

"For Christ's sake, spit it out!"

"Yes, sir. They came upon a Taliban interrogation team preparing, I'm informed, to raze this village I referred to. They were likely seeking information on our assets in the field."

"And your people engaged?"

"Sir, technically they're CIA."

"Bullshit! They work for me. I'm their goddamned Commander-in-Chief, am I not?"

"Yes, sir. You are indeed."

"So, people died in this engagement, I presume?"

"I'm told all of the Taliban went down, along with several villagers."

"And your agents?"

Putting it back on Denham Boyd again, damn it.

"They're proceeding on their way north, sir. They managed to obtain one of the raiders' vehicles. It's obviously faster than a hike out, but they still can't safely travel during daylight."

"So, they're holed up somewhere in...where are they?"

"Kunduz Province, Mister President."

"Who comes up with these names?"

"Afghanis, I suppose."

The POTUS glared at him, then turned away. "How long until they reach the border, if that's even where they're headed?"

"No place else they could go, sir. As far as time, sundown will reach the province right around six forty-five this evening. If nothing happens after that, they could be at the Uzbek border shortly after dawn. Say half-past four o'clock tomorrow morning."

"And the difference in time between us, Boyd? I'll never get that straight."

"Time zones are tricky, Mister President. Afghanistan is eight hours and a half ahead of Eastern Standard Time."

"An extra thirty minutes? Who came up with that brainstorm?"

"I'm not sure, sir. It's rare, but you find thirty- and forty-five minute deviations in several nations of the Eastern Hemisphere: Iran, Afghanistan and India, Myanmar, Bangladesh, and down the middle of Australia."

"Jesus, what a world, eh?"

"Yes, sir."

"All right. I need you on top of this, and I mean every minute from now on."

"I understand, sir."

"Good. Because if this shit takes a nosedive, Boyd, the buck's stopping with you."

CHAPTER 9

Kunduz Province

Sara Durell woke to a rustling sound inside the old, ramshackle barn and sat up with her AK carbine ready to take down a creeping enemy.

"Just me," Jack said, turning to face her from his post beside the building's warped and sagging double doors.

"Okay."

She took her weapon with her as she scrambled out of the Toyota's backseat, feeling stiff in certain places but not minding much. The weird part was remembering and wondering if she and Jack had made a critical mistake.

Not that the word would ever get to Langley. Sara had no worries on that score, but she was a professional, took pride in that, and couldn't duck her afterthoughts that maybe Jack had been correct to start with.

If the incident between them—well, make that *two* incidents—changed their dynamic in some way, would either one of them escape Afghanistan alive?

And even if they did, would operating in the future still be possible on terms they had established since Jack signed on with the CIA for "special" high-risk missions only?

He'd been broken then, deep down, but shrinks employed by George Bush Center for Intelligence had cleared him for front-line cover ops with a proviso that he might "go overboard" and place his life at risk unnecessarily if not reined in successfully.

The problem was—had always been—controlling Jack when he was on a roll, with other lives at stake.

"Did you get any sleep?" she asked him.

"Some. I heard you sawing logs."

She checked her watch and frowned. "Your shift was done an hour ago."

He answered with a lazy shrug. "No harm, no foul."

"No company?"

"Not yet. I'm thinking this must be the farm that time forgot."

She peered out through a crack between two weathered, desiccated boards, confirming that they had about two hours left before the sun went down.

"Feel like an MRE?" she asked.

"Why not? In fact, since we've got wheels, why not make it a farewell feast?"

"You think?"

"I never liked short rations much."

"But if we get cut off..."

"A meal or two won't matter, either way," Jack said.

And there was no contesting that. If they were stopped by hostile troops of either side, the ANA or Taliban, the very last thing Sara needed to concern herself about was freeze-dried food.

"Okay," she said. "What's on the menu, then?"

They dug into their MOLLE packs and came up with five MREs, three Cody had been carrying and two from Sara, since she'd been out in the field an extra day and change.

"Something for everyone," Jack said, as they laid out the plastic packs containing chili and beans, meatballs in marinara sauce, creamy spinach fettucine, beef goulash, and lemon pepper tuna. The varied side dishes included carb-enhanced apple sauce, teriyaki beef sticks, chipotle tortillas, an apple turnover they could divide between them, and trans-fat free marble pound cake. To wash it down they had coffee, tea, and powdered cocoa.

"Gordon Ramsey, eat your heart out," Sara quipped.

"Does that make this Hell's Kitchen?" Jack inquired.

"That, or the next worst thing."

They used their flameless heaters, with some water from their two hydration packs, and made a fairly decent meal of it—if not five-star, one of the better feeds that anyone on Afghan soil was likely to enjoy tonight, aside from certain hotels under heavy guard in Kabul.

Jack hadn't mentioned anything about their recent interlude so far, and Sara hoped that he would keep it that way, operating on the same basis that had been working for them up to now.

If that held true, she thought, there was a chance that both of them just might survive.

The village, Ehsan Abarkhyl discovered, had been known as Bakht-Awar in Dari, spoken by roughly one-third of Afghanis, regarded by some as a bridge language spanning the gap between Farsi and Pashto. Abarkhyl had no clue to any meaning of the name and frankly didn't care.

From what he'd seen so far, Bakht-Awar had been thoroughly annihilated as a settlement.

It didn't take a genius to reconstruct last night's events. A flying squad of Taliban—one of their Red Units—had come upon the village while attempting to capture the spy, now thought to be a woman from America, if anyone could credit that. He had Sediq Qayoumi's word for that, after the *kus* had threatened him over the telephone, and why would Ehsan's captain lie to him?

Abarkhyl's goal now was to find out where she'd gone and who, if anyone, was aiding her escape.

The former desert village, Bakht-Awar, had been transformed into a slaughterhouse. From what Ehsan observed, he understood that the Red Unit's leader, Omar Jamalzadah, had begun interrogating peasants in the hope of learning whether anyone had seen the fleeing fugitive. Apparently, he'd met resistance from the village elder—possibly because the old man knew nothing; perhaps because he held some grudge against the Taliban—and Omar had responded with a point-blank execution.

Then, it seemed, an enemy had come out of the darkness and proceeded to annihilate the Taliban's "elite" strike force, killing the lot of them as if they were recruits attacked before learning the basic means of self-defense.

That seemed impossible, and yet the evidence was all around Ehsan Abarkhyl, lying sprawled and twisted in the sand, a few slumped near their armored vehicles, with ample evidence that automatic weapons and grenades had cut them down.

All that, and while Red Unit members had killed off a few more villagers while fighting vainly for their lives, Ehsan could find no evidence that any Talib had inflicted wounds on their aggressive enemies.

A massacre, in fact, and an embarrassment to Allah's great jihad.

Abarkhyl knew that one or more of the surprise killers had fled in a Toyota Hilux pickup stolen from the scene. Four other vehicles were present and accounted for, three ready for removal when his own team left the killing ground of Bakht-Awar, assuming all of them would start and run upon demand. If not, he had instructions to destroy them, leaving no clues for the ANA as to precisely where or when the vehicles had been acquired.

That was the easy part.

As for discovering his prey, running the killers down...

well, "north" would not be good enough.

Ehsan Abarkhyl grasped the logic of his enemies escaping to Uzbekistan, as far as that went, though he doubted that Uzbek authorities would be involved in helping the American Crusaders infiltrate Afghanistan. Ninety percent of all Uzbeks were Muslims, five percent Russian Orthodox Christians, and the remainder indeterminate. Of some 94,000 Jews counted in 1989, barely five thousand still remained.

If faith were all it took to solve Ehsan's problem...

A cry from one of his sentries distracted Abarkhyl. He turned to face the sound and saw more vehicles approaching, three of them in line, trailing pale plumes of dust. His soldiers fanned out, ready to eradicate the new arrivals on Abarkhyl's order, but he snapped at them to wait a moment longer.

When the first of three Jeep Wranglers pulled into the one-time village, Ehsan recognized its front-seat passenger, doing his best to mask the frown that came unbidden to his face.

Captain Mohammed Ali Isani of the Pakistani ISI.

And what in Allah's name could he be doing there?

"Not bad, as army rations go," Cody remarked.

"I guess not," Sara answered him. "You finished everything except the plastic bags."

"Waste not, want not."

"Until next mealtime rolls around," she said.

"If we still haven't reached the border," Jack replied, "I

think it's safe to say we won't be having any hunger pangs."

Her face and tone went serious. "You think we won't?" she asked.

"I gave up telling fortunes," Cody said. "It wasn't working out."

She pulled the magazine from her AKS-74U and double-checked its load, then slapped it back in place. Outside, advancing dusk filtered errant rays of desert sunlight beaming through the barn's innumerable cracks and knotholes.

"Are we set, then?"

"Just about to top off the gas tank," said Jack, as he removed a jerrycan from the Toyota's bed, removed the pickup's gas cap, and began refueling from the olive drab five-gallon can. When he was done, roughly a gallon still remained inside the jerrycan, another five inside its twin.

"All good to go," he said.

Sara was peering at her GPS transponder, reading off coordinates.

"Looks like we've got another hundred miles to go," she said. "That's as the crow flies, staying clear of highways."

"Over rough terrain," Jack said, "that could take us three hours, maybe more."

He didn't have to add that he was calculating travel time without vehicular breakdowns or any other interruption that could leave them traveling by foot again. In that case, they'd regret the splurge with their remaining MREs—or else they wouldn't be alive to give a damn.

"We'd best be careful, then," Sara replied. "You want to flip for who drives first?"

"Suits me," he said, and dug out an afghani coin.

Instead of heads and tails, the five-afghani coin—roughly equivalent an American nickel—displayed a domed palace on one side, framed by scimitars. On the reverse, an eagle spread its wings inside a wreath of some kind.

"You want the bird or swords?" he asked.

"I'll let you have the bird," Sara replied, smiling.

"Why am I not surprised?"

"It's like you know me."

Cody didn't answer that but flipped the coin and let it drop onto the barn's dirt floor.

"Looks like you got the bird," Sara observed.

"The story of my life."

"I'll spell you in…what? Ninety minutes?"

"Sounds all right."

Afghanis drive on the left side of roads, such as they are, which meant that the Toyota's steering wheel was on the right. Worldwide, some 65 percent of all nations and territories mandate right-hand drive, most of the lefties being members of the former British Empire plus Japan. Jack climbed into the driver's seat and propped his AK-107 up against the door immediately to his right, while Sara rode shotgun.

The Toyota Hilux had a two-liter "3Y" engine with a five-speed manual transmission, capable of halfway decent highway speeds, but that assumed that drivers would be traveling on halfway decent highways. Over often-rocky desert ground, damage to tires, suspension, tailpipes, oil pans and the like was commonplace, a constant headache during off-road travel, even when the pickups had been "built to last" in advertising terms.

Night-vision gear permitted driving without headlights, though it meant a further sacrifice of speed. That didn't bother Cody, as ten hours of darkness lay between sundown and breaking dawn. Even if they were forced to creep across the landscape at ten miles per hour, they could make the Uzbek border by sunrise.

The trick, he realized, would lie in getting there alive.

Washington, D.C.

It was lunchtime but Denham Boyd had lost his appetite. He was brown-bagging it, a homemade sandwich that he had been looking forward to—salami and Swiss cheese on rye, with mustard, tomato and onions—but now he couldn't face it, as his boss's words echoed inside his head.

If this shit takes a nosedive, Boyd, the buck's stopping with you.

He had no doubt the POTUS meant exactly what he'd said. At that level of politics, self-preservation was the only true religion. Never mind about the photo ops in church, at "prayer breakfasts", weddings, funerals, whatever. No one made it to the top in Washington or any other nation's capital without honing their CYA skills to an art form.

And those letters didn't stand for the Chantilly Youth Association, much less "See-ya" as employed on social media.

Well, two could play that game, though Boyd freely admitted that he'd been outclassed. There was a reason why he set his cell phone on "RECORD" whenever he was summoned to the Oval Office, as a hedge against convenient lapses in the presidential memory if outside Denham's control went south and he was left holding the leaky bag.

Not this kid. Not today. Not ever.

Boyd considered himself loyal, oath-bound without regard to whoever America's electorate decided should inhabit the White House for four years at a stretch, but he wasn't about to be the next John Dean or Ollie North. If push came down to shove, Boyd wasn't falling on his sword to save a man who treated him with utter disregard.

Sara Durell might have been shocked if she could read his mind, or maybe not. Together, they inhabited a nether world of secrets, lies, and extralegal actions executed in the name of national security, where things got done because they *had to*, or the consequences would be vastly more severe than simply sitting on one's hands to wait it out.

And when push came to deadly wet work, there was always someone standing by to handle that. Jack Cody was a prime example of the species, even if Boyd sometimes pondered whether Jack was altogether rational.

He wasn't crazy, though...unless it might be crazy like a fox.

So far, whatever dirty job was handed to him, Cody had come out on top. When it was time to literally save the world, he was the Land of Freedom's go-to guy, prepared to duke it out with any adversary, no holds barred.

But someday, somewhere, he was bound to drop the ball. Cody had lost his family already, made no secret of the fact that he had lost all fear of death the moment he received that ghastly news.

But laughing in the face of death didn't make anyone immune to it.

If Cody failed this time around, if Sara went down with him, Boyd expected that his own head would be next up on the chopping block.

And if it came to that, whoever tried to take him down was in for a surprise.

Kunduz Province

"You've found it, then, I see," Captain Isani of the ISI declared as he approached, stating the obvious.

"Some time ago," replied Ehsan Abarkhyl, swallowing an urge to snap at his unwelcome visitor.

"And what, if anything, have you discovered?" asked Isani.

"Only what you see, Captain." A measure of respect was still required, to keep the flow of arms and cash from Pakistan continuing, but Ehsan did not have to like it.

"Ah. So, nothing, eh? What of survivors from the village, then?"

"Missing," said Ehsan. "Wherever they've gone, they must be hours ahead of us and left no tracks."

"Have you deployed your drones, Lieutenant?" Tagging Ehsan with a lower rank that had no counterpart or meaning to the Taliban.

"We have," Abarkhyl said, omitting any mention of Isani's rank this time. "But northward, in pursuit of the Crusader fugitives."

"You speak in plurals now?" Isani cocked one bushy eyebrow as he lit a cigarette and dropped the match, letting it burn out in the sand.

"We have determined that at least two killers were involved," Ehsan confirmed. "Their weapons were of different calibers, based on the cartridge casings left behind."

"You seek a man *and* woman, then?"

"Apparently, based on a very brief, one-sided conversation on the telephone."

Isani blew a cloud of smoke toward Ehsan and remarked, "You may know that I first proposed a female agent's possible involvement in this case."

"Congratulations," Abarkhyl replied, sidestepping a temptation to smirk. "Unfortunately, that does not help us to locate either fugitive."

"But you are searching to the north?"

"As ordered by Captain Sediq Qayoumi. Yes."

"In the belief that they are headed for Uzbekistan?"

"Where else?" Ehsan inquired. "The vehicle they captured absolutely went away in that direction. We've confirmed it."

"But the weather, as I understand, has foiled your searching."

"So far," Abarkhyl amended. "We remain hopeful."

"Of course. But hope is so…ephemeral, don't you agree?"

"I much prefer it to defeatism."

"And wisely so. However, if the choice were mine—"

Abarkhyl saw where he was going and anticipated it. "You may suggest a plan to intercept them. I am pleased to say that operation is proceeding as we speak."

The shaggy eyebrow rose again. "Indeed?"

"A second Red Unit is stationed closer to the Uzbek border. Following an order from my captain, they are presently deploying as an obstacle to travel northward. No one should be able to avoid them."

" 'Should be'," came the Pakistani's echo, rife with skepticism.

"Nothing in this life is absolutely certain," Ehsan said, "except the fact of death."

"And dedication to Allah," Isani added.

"Ah. If that were only true for all Afghans and those they have to tolerate in daily life."

Captain Isani smiled at that, but it seemed forced, a strained expression. "I suspect you are a man to watch, Lieutenant," he replied.

"You flatter me," Abarkhyl said this time, "with rank that is not mine."

"Things change in war, and rapidly," Isani said. "You might consider offering a prayer to Allah that your drones and interception troops succeed before sunrise. And try your best to get this mess cleaned up before Kabul's troopers arrive."

Baghlan Province

"So, he was there?" Sediq Qayoumi asked into the sat phone.

"Yes, sir. But he's gone now." Static crackled behind Ehsan Abarkhyl's reply, perhaps some kind of interference from the atmosphere. "Did you know he was coming?"

"I suspected it but saw no reason to alarm you, if I was mistaken."

"I don't trust him, Captain."

"Nor should you, Ehsan. He's Pakistani, after all. A servant of their government, and therefore suspect automatically."

Ehsan might have replied that they were all supposed to be on Allah's side, but he wisely refrained, allowing silence to evoke Qayoumi's next remark.

"What have you learned from the ScanEagle drones?" he asked his second in command.

"Nothing so far," Abarkhyl said. "We still have time, sir."

"But it's running short, you must agree."

"Of course."

"Assuming that they kept the pickup truck, what would you estimate as their top speed?"

"Across the open desert, with its hazards? Fifteen miles per hour, using headlights. If they turn those off for safety's sake, no more than ten, possibly less."

"And they'll have started out at dusk, yes?"

"Almost certainly. If they were traveling by daylight…"

"They would already have reached the Uzbek border. Yes.

I understand."

"We'll stop them yet, sir."

"If we don't, there will be...repercussions."

"Understood."

"Where has Isani gone?"

"He didn't share that information, sir," Ehsan replied. "But I suspect he's headed back your way."

"Again, as I suspected."

"He has armed men with him, Captain."

"From the ISI?" Sediq inquired.

"We were not introduced. Their uniforms had no insignia, of course, but they obeyed his orders."

"Did they wear maroon berets, by any chance?"

"No, sir."

The headgear that Qayoumi had referred to was a trademark of the Pakistan Army's Special Service Group, mandated and tasked with aspects of unconventional warfare including counter-terrorism, direct actions, foreign internal defense and reconnaissance. Specific SSG tasks covered combat search and rescue, counter-proliferation, military hostage rescue, psywar operations, peacekeeping missions, security assistance and enemy manhunts, like the one ongoing now.

Command and control of the SSG fell under the Pakistan Army's Strategic Forces Command, and its personnel were often recruited into ISI's Covert Action Division upon retirement from active duty.

Then again, Isani might be backed by mercenaries with no loyalty beyond their next paycheck.

"If Isani and his people should return—"

Ehsan anticipated him, saying, "I shall be cautious, sir."

"A wise choice, Ehsan. Be prepared for anything that may arise."

"And we shall carry out our mission at all costs."

"I would expect no less."

"Sir, if I may say…"

"Yes? Go on."

"Captain Isani indicated—no, *implied*—that he might be dissatisfied with your performance, sir. I only mention it, you understand—"

"To keep me briefed on a potential danger. I appreciate your candor, Ehsan."

"We all fight in Allah's name, sir. And I feared that he might raise the subject with you later, trying to suggest a plot against you on my part."

"At this point, I put nothing past him."

"I believe that's wise, sir."

"And I thank you for your loyalty, Ehsan. *As-Salaam-Alaikum.*"

"*Wa-Alaikum-Salaam,*" said Abarkhyl, then broke the sat phone connection.

Loyalty, indeed.

Sediq Qayoumi had faith in his field commander—to a point. He trusted that Ehsan would do his best to track and catch or kill the fugitives he was pursuing, but a range of personal considerations might distract him in the process. Blandishment from their purported ISI supporter might confuse him or encourage Abarkhyl to think Qayoumi had some grudge against him, nurtured privately. Isani might even persuade Sediq's right hand that a betrayal of their trust was somehow in his own best interest, even an assurance of survival.

If he caught the Pakistani at it, then Isani's days were numbered. Qayoumi could count them on the fingers of one hand.

And it would not disturb him in the least to eliminate the *ghul san* when it suited him.

Kunduz Province

Driving through near-pitch darkness, navigating by his AN/AVS-6 night-vision goggles, wasn't quite the picnic armchair warriors might imagine. Jack Cody saw the Afghan desert etched in shades of gray, knowing that if he drove too fast, he might not spot a wash or gully in their path until driven the Toyota Hilux into it nose-first.

Airbags would be small consolation in that case, even if neither he nor Sara suffered broken noses or some other injury from the impact. Losing their ride—a broken axle, blown-out radiator, ruptured oil pan or whatever—would be on a par with major trauma to their bodies.

Walking the last eighty miles or so to reach the Uzbek border was no longer viable, with hostile troops and tracking drones in hot pursuit, particularly now that they'd consumed the last of their accumulated MREs.

Better to take it slow and easy with the pickup, knowing

they had long, dark hours still ahead of them, and reach the border in one piece.

What happened after that was anybody's guess, as likely down to Fate or luck as any kind of thought-out plan.

Sara was counting on a sat phone contact when they'd nearly reached their destination, hoping that a chopper might be sent to fetch them, but the borderlands they sought were volatile, to say the least. The Afghan guards might lean toward negligence, but if authorities in Kabul issued orders to obstruct them, that could change within a heartbeat. Only weeks ago, in January 2016, border troops had opened fire on NATO's Resolute Support mission advisors, losing one Afghani soldier who was killed, another wounded in the brief exchange.

Beyond that, should they make it past the half-assed guards on their side of the borderline, Uzbekistan's watchmen were notorious hardcases, ramped up and ready for anything headed their way. Jack couldn't picture Sara or himself surviving such a confrontation, any way it played out in his mind while the dark desert came to meet him, then retreated in his rearview mirror.

And that could be a major problem, sure.

Jack made no bones about the fact that he was ready to go whole-hog every time he hit the field, not terribly concerned about his own survival when the smoke cleared, but his cavalier approach to life and death didn't extend to Sara. He was bent on getting her back home alive and well, no matter that he'd taken on his job himself, without official sanction, much less a specific order from upstairs.

And if he failed, what would that mean?

On one hand, Cody wouldn't know it, being dead himself. But on the off chance that some kind of ultimate reward or penalty lay waiting for him on the Other Side, he didn't want to exit from his life a loser, having fumbled on the one-yard line.

Sara Durell deserved better, no matter what Jack thought about himself.

And if a last-ditch screwup kept him from a hypothetical reunion with his wife and kids, improbable as that might be... well, failure then became unthinkable. Intolerable.

"Tired of driving yet?" she asked him, from the shotgun seat.

"Not yet," Jack said. "You want to catch some z's, go on ahead. I'll wake you when I need a break."

"Well, if you're sure..."

"As can be," Jack replied. And knew, in fact, he wasn't sure of anything right now.

CHAPTER 10

Kunduz Province

Sandjar Zadran had been a Red Unit commander for the better part of nineteen months. Within that time, he'd led attacks on ANA and NATO units, kidnapped witless archaeologists from France, extorting ransom from their government despite its non-negotiation bluster, and had executed village elders who insisted on supporting President Ashraf Ghani.

Tonight's assignment, though, might be the one that gave Zadran a breakthrough in his service to the Taliban.

Crusader fugitives were on the run after a spying mission meant to undermine Allah's holy jihad. If what he had been told was accurate, one of the infiltrators was a woman, both likely dispatched from the Great Satan known as the United States. A squad of Western troops had tried to rescue them, and while the soldiers had been slain, the two invaders had rebounded with a massacre of freedom fighters in some worthless village to the south of where Zadran's unit was presently deployed.

If he could capture them alive, Mawlawi Hibatullah Akhundzada himself might pin a medal onto Zadran's khaki uniform, promoting him to bigger, better things.

Conversely, if Zadran was forced to kill the fugitives, at least he hoped to have some time alone with the female, to teach her what a grave mistake she'd made by meddling in Afghanistan.

Zadran's instructions from Ehsan Abarkhyl claimed the runners would attempt to reach Uzbekistan, but Zadran's unit was patrolling the desert through which he estimated they would have to pass before reaching that goal. They were spread thin, but any sighting would produce a message summoning the Red Unit to gather and cut off the enemy's retreat.

At present, Zadran's men were watching for a pickup truck stolen from their dead comrades during last night's massacre. If still in operation, it was said to be a four-year-old Toyota Hilux painted shades of desert camouflage, not mounting any weapons, though the spies apparently had brought their own. Around three dozen members of the Taliban were dead already, since the hunt began, not even mentioning cruise missile strikes that had resulted from whatever information the Crusaders had collected early on.

They owed a debt of blood to those they'd wronged, and Sandjar Zadran meant to see it paid before sunrise. Failing at that, he was prepared to sacrifice his own life and the lives of all his men.

But first, they had to narrow down the search, locate their prey, and strike before the runners could escape.

Two fugitives, and one of them a female. How much trouble could they be?

Enough, it seemed, to infiltrate Captain Sediq Qayoumi's headquarters, assassinate one of his guards, and then escape with vital information that brought missiles raining down upon selected targets in Afghanistan. Enough, when that was done, to slaughter an entire Red Unit in the field and slip away unscathed.

Sandjar Zadran would not permit that travesty to be perpetuated on his watch. Allah's most sacred cause was on the line, coupled with basic human pride. If two Crusaders—one of them a filthy *kus,* inferior by nature—could run rings around the Taliban, killing its troops at will, who else would seek to emulate their crimes?

Zadran imagined that the very future of the movement was at stake, and he was tasked to save it from an ignominious demise. The scum of ISIL would be gloating even now, concocting ways to infiltrate Afghanistan, supplant the Taliban on its home turf.

But not tonight, or any other night while Sandjar Zadran was on guard.

He was the teacher, ready to instruct his adversaries in a lesson they would not live to pass on.

Sara Durell was dozing when Jack saw the headlights up

ahead, still easily a mile or more ahead of their blacked-out Toyota. Reaching over with his left hand, he gave her a nudge and startled her awake.

"What's up?" she asked, then saw the lights herself. "Oh, hell."

"It stands to reason they'd be waiting for us, right?"

"I know. But I was hoping we could slip around them, somehow."

"We can stop and try to wait them out," Cody replied. "They haven't seen us yet, as far as I can tell."

"It's tempting," Sara answered. "But if someone's in for a surprise, I'd rather it be them."

"I count five sets of headlights. You?"

"The same. Reminds me of the village."

"We had an advantage there."

"Distraction. No need to remind me, Jack."

"Okay. Now, we've got surprise."

"Unless they've got night-vision gear, that is."

"Maybe they do, but it's negated by their headlights."

"Compromised, at least," she said. "Okay, so what's your plan?"

"Drive up on them and take advantage of the night, long as we can."

She mulled that over for a long moment, then said, "All right. I don't see any way around it, short of sitting here until they go away."

"Assuming that they do."

"You've sold me." Sara raised the AKS-74U from her lap

and flicked its safety switch into the "OFF" position. "Ready when you are."

Jack didn't have to check his AK-107. He already knew its magazine was full, a live round ready in the chamber, and a 40mm HE round inside the under-barrel GP-25 grenade launcher. His other weapons, likewise, were ready to rock and roll upon a second's notice.

"I'll take it easy, heading in," he said, "unless they spot us."

"Less noise that way," she agreed. "And we don't need a busted axle."

"Roger that."

Pegging the group of headlights at a mile away, maybe a little farther, Cody thought the pace he had been holding since they'd left the desert farmstead ought to put them within fighting range and would close the distance by roughly five hundred yards inside a minute. If their adversaries hadn't spotted them by then, he'd try another minute on for size and be prepared to fight the moment someone noticed their pickup's approach.

"What say I light them up at half a mile and gun it?" Cody asked.

She frowned at that idea, then shrugged and answered, "Driver's rules."

"Okay, then. If they spot us first…"

"Stop, drop and roll," she said. "I know the drill."

"I thought that's only if your clothes catch fire."

"Could happen."

"Sure, but—"

"Just drive, Jack."

He drove. Straight toward the not-so-distant headlights, navigating through his AN/AVS-6 goggles. It was dicey, seeing how far he could press their luck, but Jack saw no alternative and Sara had signed off on the impulsive plan.

Which wouldn't serve as any consolation if it got them killed.

They'd covered some two hundred yards of desert when a spotlight flared in front of them, swept past their pickup truck, then instantly reversed its course to pin the Hilux in its glare.

"Okay," Jack muttered, pushing up his goggles so the high beam wouldn't blind him. "How about Plan B?"

"I have them!" one of Sandjar Zadran's soldiers shouted, focusing his spotlight on a pickup truck advancing toward the Talib skirmish line.

Zadran shoved another of his men aside, seized the spotlight mounted on his Jeep, and swung its beam toward the approaching Toyota, pinning it dead-center in a blinding white X. He glimpsed two passengers, a man behind the pickup's steering wheel—and yes! That *was* a woman in the front passenger's seat.

"Stand ready!" he commanded, shouting it along the line of vehicles. "Remember, we must try to capture one of them alive, at least."

None of his men responded verbally, but Zadran heard the

click-clack of their weapons being cocked by anxious hands.

Was it ridiculous to think that he could capture either of the spies for questioning? Perhaps, but he was bound to try—and having bawled the order out for all to hear, he had covered himself with headquarters in case something went wrong.

"Shoot at the tires first!" he commanded. "Carefully! Remember that we are required to take—"

Zadran never completed what he'd meant to say. Mid-sentence, the Toyota's female passenger leaned from her window and unleashed a burst of automatic fire from a stubby Kalashnikov of some kind, either a carbine of submachine gun. At the same time, her driver accelerated, charging toward the Taliban convoy, firing with a pistol in his right hand from his open window toward the vehicles lined up in front of him.

At once, gunfire erupted up and down the Talib caravan, weapons ranging from AK rifles to a heavy NSV machine gun mounted on a Humvee captured from a NATO unit six months earlier, repainted, and drafted to serve on Allah's side. The concussive sound of 12.7mm rounds eclipsed all other calibers along the firing line, hurling downrange projectiles weighing fifty-five grams each—twelve to a pound of lead and copper traveling at half a mile per second through the night.

Zadran was sighting down the barrel of his own AK-74 when he saw the first rounds strike their target. As he rushed to meet them, the Toyota's driver had switched on his own high beams, disorienting some of Zadran's men, but both headlights were quickly blasted from their sockets, first the left and then the right blacked out. Next, bullets pierced the charging pickup's grill and radiator, hammering its engine block, while steam and smoke erupted from beneath its hood.

"That's it!" Zadran cried out. "But watch the—"

He'd intended to say "windscreen," but just then the pickup's tinted glass imploded, showering the front-seat passengers with pebbles predesigned to cause a minimum of injury. The spray of fractured glass forced the Toyota's driver to recoil, foot easing off the accelerator, while the Hilux took a storm of drumming hits.

"Lower your aim!" Zadran commanded, but in truth it seemed no one was listening. His men kept pouring rounds into the stolen pickup, while its passengers returned fire, toppling first one of his men, immediately followed by another and another.

"*Fa'iesha loor!*" he cursed, then shouted at his soldiers, "Watch your aim! We must—"

Before he could complete the order, both front doors of the Toyota opened and its passengers bailed out, rolling through desert sand and gravel. The Hilux, aiming straight at Zadran's Jeep, still taking hits as it rolled on at ramming speed.

Sara Durell rolled over twice, then came up firing with her AK carbine, picking off two enemies whose rifles tracked her from the flat bed of a battered Afghan Army truck. One of them toppled over backwards, while the other did a jerky little dance, twirling around, the last rounds out of his Kalashnikov wasted on open sky.

A tracer round from the Taliban's 12.7mm heavy machine gun sizzled past her face, close enough that its heat singed Sara's cheek, and then she saw the bullet-riddled Toyota pickup collide with a Jeep in the jihadi convoy. Impact sent the Jeep's occupants tumbling to earth, then its fuel tank exploded on impact, torching one of the *mujahideen* as he fell.

"How's that for hellfire, asshole?" Sara muttered as she ducked another near-miss round and dropped her carbine's empty rust-colored magazine, snapping a fresh one into place. Another slug pelted her flank with desert sand, but she was long past feeling it.

At least two dozen more jihadists had their hearts set on destroying her right now, a fate immensely preferable to live capture as a hostage for their warped amusement and production of their propaganda videos. If it came down to death or playing hostage, Sara knew she'd gladly choose the option Cody had been chasing since he lost his wife and children to an act of mindless savagery.

But not if she could help him kill the Talibs first.

As if on cue, Cody fired off one of his 40mm rounds, striking the Humvee with its turret-mounted heavy machine gun. The vehicle was armored, but that didn't seem to help much as the blast rocked it on its suspension, throwing off the gunner's aim just long enough for Jack to drop him with a burst of 5.45mm rounds, nearly decapitating him before his corpse slumped over, out of sight.

Sara couldn't exactly say the tide had turned yet, in their

favor, but the insurgents were wavering, some bailing out of vehicles and breaking for the darkness as their discipline deserted them. She tracked a couple of the runners, dropped one with a three-round burst across his pelvis that ensured he'd never walk again if he survived, then hit the other with a brisk tattoo between his heaving shoulder blades that planted him face down into the dust.

The first man she had shot was screaming and she left him to it, seeking other targets in the night. Another 40mm round from Cody's "Bonfire" launcher turned the cab of a Ford Ranger LTV into a blazing crematorium, the pickup's erstwhile driver shrieking as he fried behind the steering wheel.

By now, the battleground was redolent of gun smoke, high explosives, blood, and roasting flesh. If Sara hadn't been caught up in fighting for her life, it might have sickened her, but as it was, the stark aroma only served to fuel her rage. Each well-aimed round she fired struck home, coming to rest in flesh and bone, unleashing cries of pain.

And it was music to her ears.

She didn't stop to ask herself if there was something wrong with her, no more than any other warrior locked in mortal combat would. The cowards cut and ran when shit got heavy. Those who stayed to fight out were made of sterner stuff, and if that hardness was achieved by sacrificing what polite society called "conscience", well, so be it.

Standards of what passed for "civilized" changed with the seasons, flapping in the wind like sheets pinned to a clothesline. The hard realities of life and death were something else entirely, something many people never understood until they faced their bitter end.

This battle hadn't reached that end, by any means, but they were getting closer to it by the second. When the smoke cleared, if she wasn't standing in a field of corpses with Jack Cody at her side, Sara Durell had made her peace with Death.

Jack Cody thumbed a 40mm buckshot cannister into his AK-107's under-barrel launcher, just in time to meet a quartet of his enemies as they rushed toward him, firing automatic weapons from their hips.

The Talibs' haste and failure to try actually aiming spoiled their first attempt to kill Jack, and the *banzai* charge they tried next only hampered that attempt further. Jack could have chopped them down with three-round bursts from his Kalashnikov, but he was all about conserving ammunition—and, frankly, he'd seized upon the opportunity to try out an experiment.

Why not?

The round he'd chosen was an M576, designated a "grenade" although its contents consisted of twenty buckshot pellets weighing an aggregate twenty-four grams. In U.S. military tests, thirteen of those pellets lodged within a sixty-inch circle when fired from forty yards. The other seven pellets might go anywhere, strike anyone or anything, making the cannister a kind of deadly bonus package.

Cody squeezed the Bonfire launcher's trigger and hung

on, watching the impact of his buckshot slugs down range. Designed for close quarters combat—clearing buildings, bunkers, and trenches, or fighting in thick vegetation—each of the twenty pellets was equivalent to double-ought buckshot, roughly .33 caliber. Up close and personal, the net result was human devastation.

In an eyeblink, Cody saw his adversaries virtually shredded, blown away with five or six hits each, spread out between their throats and knees. It seemed as if they'd run into a cloud of crimson mist, invisible before they reached it, bursting out of nowhere then and painting the four runners bright fire-engine red. They died without a whimper, spun and dropped together in a snarl of bloodied torsos, arms and legs.

Ghastly, but damned effective, too.

If given half a chance, Jack reckoned he could keep that up all night, but in the same split-second he knew time was running short. With thirty-odd combatants on the other side, the chances of one reaching out by radio or sat phone with a bid for reinforcements was a lead-pipe cinch. The good news: there'd been no reports so far of any Taliban air force existing, so whatever help might be forthcoming had to travel overland through darkness, risking interception by erratic ANA patrols.

The answer was to wrap this up as soon as possible and get a move on toward the Uzbek border while some portion of the night remained to cover them.

And they would absolutely need new wheels.

Get busy, then, Jack thought, and fed his *Kostyor* launcher yet another deadly buckshot round.

Watching his soldiers die around him—some screaming, some others dropping silently to bloodstained soil—Sandjar Zadran experienced a sense of panic that he hadn't felt since childhood, when Soviet agents dragged his father from their village home in Ghazni Province to interrogate him about aiding *mujahideen* guerillas.

Zadran's father had never returned nor been heard from again, Zadran displaced with his mother and two older siblings, taught to hate all Russians and the Afghan government with its corrupt collaborators. That had led him to this present time and place, feeling the same old fears again.

Except that now he was a man, a soldier in his own right, and he would not yield to childish terrors.

True, he'd almost died short moments earlier, in the explosion of his Jeep on impact by the Hilux pickup stolen from his murdered Talib brethren just last night. His superficial wounds still seeped with blood, their pain distracting him, but Zadran knew what he must do.

First thing, report contact with their elusive enemies to Ehsan Abarkhyl at regional headquarters.

Second, finish off the two Crusader demons who were bent on wiping out his Red Unit commandos and himself.

Zadran's fingers were slippery with blood and perspiration as he palmed the sat phone, speed-dialing Ehsan's number, sifting through his jumbled thoughts to choose the proper words of explanation. He must keep it short, succinct, then get back to his men while Abarkhyl arranged for reinforcements, likely forced to seek approval in advance from Captain Qayoumi.

Zadran had come to recognize the benefits of military discipline, but there were still occasions when it wasted too much precious time.

Like now.

Zadran hunched down behind a four-ton Afghan Army truck, captured the better part of two years earlier, converted into use for Allah's holy cause, and listened to the hum of outer space before his call rang through to Ehsan's headquarters in Bamyan Province. It still felt bizarre, bouncing the call off a satellite to reach a person located barely 240 miles by road, but the requirements of security took precedence over what Zadran sometimes saw as common sense.

Gunfire continued raging all around him as Zadran counted the not-so-distant rings on Ehsan's end of the phone line.

One...two...

The steady firing, punctuated by explosions, told Zadran their enemies were still alive and fighting, with no sign of giving up.

A man's voice answered midway through the third ring, cautiously inquiring, "Who is this?"

It was not Ehsan's voice, another damned delay. Zadran identified himself and ordered, "Put Ehsan Abarkhyl on the line at once!"

"He's unavailable," the faceless idiot replied. "I'll take a message, sir."

"A message? *Kona ke de mandam!* Have you lost your mind?"

A shadow loomed above Zadran. He glanced up, almost cringing, to find Fazalur Noorani, their ISI agent assigned by headquarters, asking, "What do they say?"

"Not now, you idiot!" Zadran snapped back at him.

And in his ear, the man who'd answered his call said, "As you wish, then," before he cut the link.

"*Karh bachi!*" Zadran raged. "*Ghul ukhra!*" He might well have launched a wild kick at Noorani, but some heavy flying object struck the Pakistani's chest just then, knocking him back a pace and dropping to the ground between them.

Zadran stared down at the hand grenade with barely time enough to scream.

"All dead?" Sara Durell inquired.

"Unless somebody got away," Cody replied.

"They didn't," she said. "I was watching." Thinking he'd no doubt been watching, too, but could have been distracted partway through the firefight.

"Feel like checking bodies?" Cody answered back, instead.

"And picking up another ride. Ours isn't going anywhere."

Not since he'd used it for a rolling land torpedo, but at least the pickup truck had died in a good cause, helping to save their lives.

It wasn't pleasant, checking out the Talib corpses—those

that were intact, at least, and not burned to a crisp—but Sara recognized it as a chore they'd skipped after the village massacre last night, and she'd regretted that once they were on the move, too late to turn around and get it done.

Looking for what?

She didn't know yet but would recognize it if she found something.

Taliban fighters rarely carried any personal I.D. for various reasons. Distribution of electronic Afghan identity cards called *e-Tazkira* had started in May 2018, with President Ghani and First Lady Rula receiving the first two cars issued. The plastic cards included a bearer's photograph, name and other personal info, printed in English, Dari and Pashto, plus a gold-plated contact chip. Cards were valid for five or ten years, depending on the purchase price—starting at ten afghanis—theoretically displaying proof of identity, residency and citizenship.

As if.

Within a day or two of the first *e-Tazkira* being issued, counterfeiters had been cranking out their own for buyers who objected to their names and other data being logged on applications kept forever by the Ministry of Interior. Drug smugglers were among the first recipients of phony cards, along with certain various jihadists on the nation's ever-growing WANTED list.

Talibs who spurned the cards might do so for various reasons: as an act of contempt for Kabul's ruling government and occupying troops; to save some cash; or simply since the cards were not yet mandatory. Checking corpses for them likely was a waste of time, but still...

On her fifth corpse Sara found something she didn't expect. Called out to Jack, "I've got a Pakistani here."

"Oh, yeah?"

He hurried over and she handed him the dog tags she had lifted from a youngish dead man, worn around his neck. "Surprising that he'd carry these," she said.

"I'll say."

Jack squinted at the tags by dying firelight from a nearby burning vehicle. She knew he didn't speak or read any of Pakistan's five official languages among dozens of others—Pashto, Punjabi, Saraiki, Sindhi and Urdu—but there was no mistaking the stamped ISI logo, consisting of a spiral-horned Markhor goat, Pakistan's national animal, dating a snake in front of a shield bearing the Muslim star and crescent, plus the agency's full name printed in English.

"An 'advisor', then," Jack said.

Sara filled in the air quotes on her own. Replied, "Or someone's puppeteer."

"Same thing."

"You want to leave the bodies as they are?"

"No point in wasting gasoline," she said. "Let's take the tags with us and find a ride. I'd like to get the hell away from here before we start attracting company."

CHAPTER 11

Kunduz Province

Jack was driving when they left the latest killing ground, pleased with the vehicle they had agreed on, barely damaged in the firefight that had left some of the other Talib rides burned down to smoking toast.

This time they had a Husky TSV—*Tactical Support Vehicle*—manufactured by Navistar International, formerly International Harvester. More than three hundred Huskies had deployed with British troops since 2009, serving as London's answer to the Humvee, and at least a few, this one included, had been captured by the Muslim enemy.

The Husky was "lightly" armored, meaning keep your fingers crossed, and powered by a MaxxForce D6.0L V8 engine that generated 340 horsepower, achieving a top speed of seventy miles per hour, powered by any NATO single-fuel derivative. To beat any road hazards short of mines or trenches, the

Husky ran on Hutchinson wheels with a bead lock retention system and Michelin 395/85R20 radials supported by a Dana central inflation device.

Overall, an upgrade from the Hilux that had saved their lives last night and served them as a semi-guided missile in their latest skirmish with the Taliban and ISI. Jack naturally didn't fool himself into believing they could manage top speed to the Uzbek border. Half that would be super lucky, driving through the dark, and at twenty miles per hour they should still beat sunrise to the border, even with the time they'd lost fighting another battle in transit.

As long as they didn't get ambushed again or bogged down by some other distraction en route.

Sara shifted in the Husky's front passenger seat and asked Cody, "How are you holding up?"

"I've got a few miles still left in me."

"Good to know. But you've been driving for a while. You need a breather. I could take it for a while."

Cody glanced at the Husky's dashboard clock, set to Afghani time, and answered, "Maybe in another hour or so. I'll let you know."

"Sounds good." She pulled her sat phone from one of the many cargo pockets on her desert camo uniform. "Meanwhile, I'd better touch base while I can."

"I can pull over if you want. Give you some privacy," Jack said.

"Not necessary. Just don't fall asleep and crack us up."

"I'll do my best."

Another call to Denham Boyd in Washington. Jack didn't envy Sara's being on a White House leash, although he guessed the same could logically be said of him. Without his government connection, there would be no missions in his future, nothing but an endless span of empty days and nights until he got fed up and put a pistol in his mouth.

Not in the hope of a reunion with his murdered wife and children, mind you. Cody had no faith in that, even if certain tearful dreams gave him a glimpse of those he'd loved and lost, strolling through green Elysian Fields or their equivalent. That pie in the sky—make it pie à la mode—didn't fit with the things he had seen or the shit he had done in this world.

"Intelligent design"? So, who'd dreamed up the notions that included ticks and liver flukes, cancer and leprosy? Was that a sign of some Almighty's "love", or was the whole thing just a cosmic practical joke devised by some sadist?

Sara connected via outer space, and Cody tuned her out, dividing his attention between navigation with his AN/AVS-6 night-vision goggles and delving into cosmic thoughts that ultimately took him nowhere.

If there was a Great Beyond, against all odds, he wasn't sure how he might fit in with the rules and regulations that applied there. Life on Earth had been a challenge for Cody in that regard, despite being inured to military discipline while he was on the Pentagon's payroll. Still, many babies had gone out with the bathwater, so to speak, and now that he was taking kill-or-be-killed missions for the CIA…well, let's just say that anything and damned near everything was possible.

He was aware of Sara hanging up on Washington only when she turned toward him in her seat, saying, "I have an update, if that helps."

"So, what's the plan for crossing over?" Jack replied.

"I hope you mean the crossing the border," Sara quipped. "Boyd says that he'll have people watching for us and they'll see what they can do. That part's in quotes."

"Terrific. Welcome to the un-plan, friends and neighbors."

"That's about the size of it."

"You know we'll never get this rig across the Friendship Bridge, right?"

"Not a chance in hell. It's never been that friendly, anyway."

"So, if your buddy drops the ball..."

"A new day and the same old crap," she said. "We improvise."

Baghlan Province

Captain Mohammed Isani of Inter-Services Intelligence had hoped a cup of herbal tea would calm his nerves, the rage he felt inside, but so far nothing seemed to help. He stared across a small card table at Sediq Qayoumi, fully conscious of the fury burning in his own dark eyes.

"One of my own men murdered now, by the Crusaders you are unable to find," he snarled. "A *hawaldar*, no less. That means a sergeant, if you're ignorant of proper military terms."

"I speak your language if required to," said Qayoumi,

speaking tersely, like a man who's just discovered a foul taste upon his tongue but can't decide upon its source.

"How nice for you," Isani sneered. "We may communicate, but do you ever understand a single word that you are told? Can you follow the simplest order without bungling it stupendously?"

Dark color rose into Sediq Qayoumi's cheeks, already swarthy in the best of moods. However he intended to reply, the Afghan held his tongue, passed through a slow ten count in silence, then said, "I did not request your sergeant to accompany our Red Unit. If you recall, *Captain,* I acquiesced to that reluctantly, at your urgent insistence."

"Because I never thought he would be killed!" Isani spat.

"Do not all soldiers take that risk? Except for those who hide behind the lines and give 'advice,' of course."

"If you're tired of working with the ISI, Sediq, for Allah's sake say so. One phone call can prevent you being troubled with advice—much less money or arms—ever again."

"It's strange that you should mention Allah, Captain, when His holy cause means little more to you or your superiors than one more opportunity to spread Islamabad's influence over other warriors."

"And by 'other warriors,' I presume you mean the sort who come to us on bended knee, with hands outstretched to grasp at any spare rupees or surplus weapons we are willing to supply? Are those the beggars who you have in mind, Sediq?"

"May I speak frankly, Captain?"

"Have you not been, up to now?"

"Aside from the Crusaders, who must die by any means available, I always strive to take a civil tone with others, even those I hold in low regard."

"And? Say your worst."

"It seems to me, at times, that your commitment to jihad is like the protestation of a *fa'iesha* claiming she is 'not that kind of woman' until money changes hands. You seek advantage in a given situation while pretending sympathy or even love, but all the while your mind is operating as a calculator."

"And remembering my enemies, let me assure you."

"This is pointless," said Qayoumi, rising from his metal folding chair. "Since you despise Afghanistan so much and think her people only worthless peasants, I suggest you leave us and return to Pakistan without delay. If your director, General Mukhtar—"

"Lieutenant General," Isani said, correcting him.

Qayoumi ducked his head in mock humility. "Forgive me, please, for undeservedly promoting him. If your *Lieutenant* General should happen to replace you, I suggest he choose an officer who hates neither his posting nor the freedom fighters he is sent to serve."

Isani marveled at the Afghan's sheer audacity but made an effort to control himself. "Sediq," he said, "if you are severing relations with the ISI you must put it in writing. I presume that your commander, Hibatullah Akhundzada, would appreciate a copy of that letter for his files as well. That should prevent him suffering from shock when no more shipments of supplies or money travel south."

"I shall indeed report our conversation, Captain, while you pack your bags and start for home."

Fearing for once the possibility that Sediq might speak honestly, Isani asked, "Is there not some way for us to resolve this impasse?"

"Only if you help retrieve the fugitives. We must prevent them from escaping to Uzbekistan at any cost."

"Agreed," Isani said. "Now, please sit down and let us draft a plan."

Kunduz Province

Sara was driving and enjoying it, at least as much as she'd enjoyed a single given moment since her penetration of Afghanistan. Jack Cody dozed beside her, fitfully, inviting speculation as to what his dreams might hold in store for him.

More likely nightmares, she supposed, if he was capable of those.

She thought about the time they'd spent together earlier, inside the old abandoned farmstead's clapped-out barn. It had surprised her, even as she welcomed unaccustomed intimacy. Part of that, she realized, was living on a knife's edge, knowing any moment could turn out to be her last.

That took her back to high school days, one lame-assed jock asking her how they'd pass the time if only he and she survived into the world's End Times. She'd laughed at him until he tried to take by force what she was unwilling to give away.

At that point, she had kicked his ass and left him gimping, sitting out the next two football games and telling friends he'd fallen off a nonexistent motorbike while stunt-driving.

As if.

From that—after another flash of Jack completely out of uniform and obviously glad to see her—Sara thought back to her last terse talk with Denham Boyd. Denham was her liaison to the White House, not an agent of the Company, and therefore suspect at the best of times. His master occupied the Oval Office, not Langley's Office of the Director, who Boyd rightly regarded as one of the president's hand-picked subordinates.

That didn't mean that Boyd could boss the DCI around, but with the full weight of the White House backing him, Sara decided that she wouldn't like to bet on who came out ahead in that horse race.

As far as whether she could personally trust Boyd with her life, the way she trusted Cody, that was still an open question. Whatever happened as they neared the border would decide that riddle for her, but she knew one thing beyond all doubt.

If Denham screwed them, left them hanging and in mortal danger, he had better hope that neither Jack nor Sara managed to survive his act of treachery.

Because whoever walked or crawled away from that would absolutely want revenge.

She pushed that thought away, displeased with the direction it was taking here. Sara's adult life had been spent—some cynics might say wasted—in pursuit of duty, honor, and whatever went along with those core values. If she had to cast all that aside, go rogue as Jack had very nearly done after he lost his family…

Scratch that. Jack hadn't *lost* the wife and kids he loved beyond all others, more than any other thing on Earth. They had been *stolen* from him in an act of savagery, and while the men responsible were dead now, Cody hadn't been the one to personally put them down.

She knew that failure, as he saw it, gnawed and rankled at him every day. He hadn't failed, of course. There was a grieving process and mortal arrangements to be made. Before he'd finished that, the slayers had been sent to their reward by other willing hands.

Still…

Did a normal person ever come to terms with such a brutal loss of loved ones? And, was Jack a "normal" person, come to that, considering his past and intimate acquaintance with grim death?

Which forced her to confront another nagging question: *Am I normal, after all?*

Washington, D.C.

One thing nobody explained when they were offering a glitzy job in government, particularly at or near the very top: one slip could land you in a world of hurt, your former "friends" pretending discovering they didn't have a single word to say on your behalf.

And when you fell from those exalted heights it was a long way down.

Sometimes the tumbling former golden boy (or girl) might even wind up serving time, while those who'd given them a shove asked vultures from the media, "Who, me?"

But Denham Boyd was in it now. He'd lobbied for his present job, even exulted when his leading competition ran afoul of undercover cops working the "public morals" beat. It was his turn at cleaning up a mess somebody else had made, halfway around the globe.

Be careful what you wish for.

On the plus side, he was dealing with two field agents who knew their stuff backwards and forward. It was pure dumb luck that Sara and her partner—dead now, and in hostile hands where he might still come back to haunt his government—had been discovered by a roving Talib sentry. Now, Sara had Jack Cody, quasi-rogue loose canon that he was, and that meant two stone killers on the job, though heavily outnumbered and outgunned.

On Boyd's end, at a safe remove from mayhem, there was work still to be done, and quickly, if he meant to save the day. He had already reached out to the State Department, which rated Uzbekistan at "Level 1", advising U.S. travelers to "exercise normal precautions". He'd touched base with U.S. Embassy Tashkent, a deputy undersecretary of something or other named Bob Esperanza, providing what details Boyd could for the problem at hand.

Esperanza had been flustered, edgy, but had checked with

someone farther up the food chain and came back to Boyd with some conditional good news. It would be risky, Bob advised—allegedly unprecedented—but the embassy could make arrangements for safe passage if Sara and Cody made it to the fabled Friendship Bridge alive, unarmed, and without Taliban guerillas breathing down their necks.

It wasn't much, but Boyd had thanked the distant functionary anyway, agreed that someone in the White House would remember his cooperation when the next review of Bob's performance rolled around.

Promises, promises.

In fact, if Esperanza pulled it off, he'd be remembered for the next few minutes by some presidential aide or other, maybe even get a form letter of commendation slipped into his personnel file, but the president would never hear of Esperanza, wouldn't even know that such a person physically existed.

That was life on Pennsylvania Avenue.

You were as good or bad as your last ranking in the media, and if Boyd's plan worked out, no journalists would ever know a thing about it.

In which case, Denham simply had to live with it, hoping that no one ever took a peek inside Pandora's box.

And if it fell apart? What, then?

First up, he could expect a pink slip from the White House, telling him his services were no longer required, either in Washington or anywhere under the widespread federal umbrella. Boyd could scrounge around for a position in state government somewhere, but he'd be leaving office with a dark cloud overhead that drizzled acid rain on any hope of nailing down a decent job in public service.

Jesus, if the "public" only knew a sliver of what happened daily in the name of national security...

Boyd couldn't even carry that thought through to a conclusion.

Would Joe Average believe it, if he knew? Would Jane Doe even give a damn? Or would they all be so invested in their cell phones, shiny baubles and their mortgage payments that they shrugged it off and looked the other way?

Democracy required people to be *involved*, to give a damn.

"Good luck with that," Boyd muttered to himself.

Two of the most involved people he knew were fighting for their lives, trying to make it through another Afghan night, and Boyd felt useless at his desk. For all the good it did, he might as well be sitting on the moon.

Kunduz Province

Latif Hosseini had no formal rank within the Taliban, wore no insignia to mark his years of service to Allah and His jihad. What he *did* have was practical experience at hunting down and killing enemies who served the heathen West.

Those skills accumulated first in training, then in deadly battle for his homeland's Muslim soul, entitled him to lead his own Red Unit. And tonight, that honor placed him on the forefront of a desperate endeavor, to prevent a pair of fugitives—Crusaders—from escaping to Uzbekistan with information that could seriously wound the Taliban.

Latif Hosseini knew the infiltrators had already wreaked their share of havoc, wiping out two teams of freedom fighters on par with his own. He knew about the U.S. missile strikes precipitated by his human prey and wished to punish them for that, as well.

Death was the least that they deserved, but his superiors demanded an attempt to take the infidels alive. Logic dictated that might not be possible, but Latif understood that he must make a good-faith effort to comply in any case.

And failing that, he would annihilate his adversaries like the vermin that they were, deserving no more mercy than a rat infected with bubonic plague.

Latif Hosseini's worry now was that he might not meet the fugitives. If they found some way to avoid him and his men, where would the final blame fall, but upon his own head?

And if that transpired, then how much longer would his head remain attached to his body?

Latif had seen men shot for less: fumbling an opportunity to kill ANA soldiers or their NATO allies; loss of critical materiel; even the crimes of getting lost while on patrol or losing critical equipment in the field. His own transgression, if it came to that, would not grant him the tender mercy of a firing squad.

Would it mean crucifixion, stoning, or a combination of the two? Would some fellow jihadist use a hacksaw or survival knife to lift his head, recording the event on video, an object lesson for recruits?

Did he possess the inner strength to meet his end without the added shame of weeping, begging for his worthless life?

Better to carry out the task that was assigned to him, while others bore the brunt of failure in his place. Glory awaited him if he succeeded. If he failed…

Ishaq Tarzi, Hosseini's second in command, approached his staff car with a hesitance reserved for those who bear bad news. Before he had a chance to speak, Latif said, "Tell me."

"Yes, sir. Nothing from the drones so far."

How was that possible? Hosseini asked, "Which quadrants are you sweeping?"

"South of here, sir, covering the land between us and the last engagement."

"They will have obtained another vehicle, Ishaq. Proceeding toward the border without transport would be tantamount to suicide."

"Yes, sir. The scanning shall continue."

"And report to me the very instant you find anything at all, no matter if it seems significant or not."

"Of course, sir."

"Remind each unit member to remain alert and ready. Anyone who fails us now has bought a one-way ticket to *Jahannam*, no respite from the flames."

"How are you holding up?" Jack asked, emerging from a dream he couldn't quite recall.

"Good," Sara replied. "I'm glad you got some rest."

You want to call it that, Jack thought, but kept it to himself. His dream had come complete with fire and blood—current events in his world, rather than a full-on nightmare.

"I can spell you," he told Sara.

"So can I." She grinned at him by dashboard light. "That's Y-O-U."

"Hilarious. You should be on the stage."

"I am. We are. The last one out of Dodge."

"There must have been a wrong turn, then," he quipped. "We're not in Kansas anymore."

"Touché. You need to stop for anything?"

"No potty breaks required, thanks."

From his seat, leaning toward Sara just a little, he could see the Husky TSV's odometer, slowly clicking away the miles of desert from the point where they had jacked their latest ride. He made it seventy-odd miles to go before they neared the Uzbek border, still a lot of blank space on the Afghan map where anything could happen.

And it likely would.

Jack put on his night-vision goggles, laid aside while he was dozing, and surveyed the wasteland up ahead. He saw no vehicles or headlights yet, the only sign of life being the brief eye shine of some swift-moving quadruped—likely a fox or jackal—as it dodged out of their path.

Good hunting, Dude, Jack thought, and almost smiled.

He wouldn't wish the same to their pursuers from the Taliban or Pakistani ISI. To them, he only wished a swift, irrevocable death.

And Jack was ready to deliver that in spades. He still had fifteen mags for his Kalashnikov, 450 rounds in all, plus nine mags for his Glock, making another 117 rounds. Add in his remaining 40mm grenades and Russian F1 frags, meaning that he could whip his weight in Asiatic wildcats in a pinch.

Unless one of Jack's adversaries dropped him first.

For backup, he had Sara and her AKS carbine and her Glock 9mm, with enough spare ammunition for a fair last stand. Jack didn't fancy dying in the Afghan outback, but when all was said and done, what difference did it make?

Realtors might rise and fall to the tune of "location, location, location", but a warrior could die anywhere—at one pole or the other, maybe straddling the equator—and still be just as dead. The only part of him or her surviving then would be within their loved ones' memories.

And Cody had no loved ones left.

Some folks might say that was a lousy way to live, but Jack simply regarded it as living.

Living on the edge, perhaps, but living, nonetheless. Until his lights went out for good, he meant to fight for what he had.

"Nothing as far as drones?" he asked.

"Not that I've heard," Sara replied.

They had been driving with their headlights off and windows down, taking advantage of the night. Jack knew the usual Boeing Insitu ScanEagle drones were less than six feet long, boasting a relatively tiny ten-foot wingspan, weighing in at less than fifty pounds. Each aircraft's two-stroke engine generated 1.5 horsepower, capable of soaring for twenty-four hours at speeds between seventy and ninety miles per hour.

The bad news for earthbound targets, the ScanEagle had a maximum service ceiling of 3.7 miles, at which its muted engine noise would be inaudible downstairs. Which didn't matter to the drone's remote-control operators, since each ScanEagle carried a ViDAR optical detection system from Sentient Vision Systems, capable of scanning some seventeen thousand square miles during an average twelve-hour mission.

The bottom line: they likely wouldn't hear a drone before it spotted them, and while the little unmanned aircraft was unarmed, it could and would broadcast coordinates that let ground troops roll out to intercept them on the desert flats.

Which meant that if their enemies had eyes on high, they couldn't hide.

But they could always fight.

CHAPTER 12

Kunduz Province

Latif Hosseini pitched his half-smoked cigarette away as Ishaq Tarzi made the short trek from his APC to Latif's staff car. This time he appeared excited, like a man with news to share.

Hosseini beat him to the punch, saying, "Good news I hope?"

"Yes, sir! I mean, I hope so, sir, although—"

"The details, Ishaq, if you don't mind."

"No, sir. That is, *yes* sir. We have drone contact with a vehicle headed this way, sir. As to the passengers…"

"What kind of vehicle?" Hosseini prodded him.

"A Husky TSV. The Brits deploy them, as you know, but we have also captured several. Reports now say that one is missing from the site of the last confrontation where Sandjar Zadran's Red Unit was eliminated."

"*Salaa allah ealayh wasalam,*" Hosseini said. Translation,

"May God honor him and grant him peace."

Ishaq answered back, "*Waealaa eayilatuh*," meaning, "And upon his family."

"Enough about the dead, now. How long should it be until they reach us here?"

Hosseini's second in command frowned slightly. "At their present cautious speed, sir, and without deviation from their present course—"

"Yes, yes. Get on with it!"

"Perhaps within the next half-hour, sir. No more than forty minutes, I would say."

"And if we go to meet them? Then how long?"

"Approximately half that time sir, if we leave at once."

"Instead of stopping to prepare a meal, you mean?"

He saw the color rise in Ishaq's cheeks. Another point scored on his top subordinate.

"Of course, sir. Shall I give the order, then?"

"That strikes me as an excellent idea."

Ishaq Tarzi gave his commander a salute of sorts, half-hearted as it seemed, then jogged away, already shouting orders to the other members of Hosseini's Red Unit. In seconds flat his men were on the move, collecting weapons, piling into dusty vehicles. There was no fire to smother, since Hosseini had forbidden any show of light that could betray their presence to the enemy.

Now that a drone had sounded the alarm of battle shaping up, concealment mattered little. Latif's convoy would advance with high-beam headlights blazing through the desert night to meet his foes and either capture them alive—still most un-likely, Hosseini believed—or else to leave them crushed and bloody in the sand.

He owed that to the other faithful Talibs they had killed, to the employees of the factory that had produced the Devil's Rain, even to the opium farmers killed or driven out of busi-ness by American cruise missiles, when their sales of poison in the west had served Allah's holy jihad.

Hosseini's enemies were also enemies of God, and they had much to answer for, in this life and the next.

And what awaited them beyond the pale? Christians be-lieved in Hell, as ardent Muslims lived in fear of *Jahannam*, but what Crusaders saw as justified, the chosen people of Allah regarded as malignant sin.

Which of them was correct?

Latif Hosseini knew that it must he his side, for Allah was the one and only God. All others were impostors, leading fools along the pathway to eternal fire.

And when they reached it, they would be in for a rude surprise.

Cody had taken over driving five miles back, hoping Sara could get some sleep, but so far, she displayed no signs of doz-ing off. He couldn't blame her in the present circumstances, but she'd spent enough time on the battlefront to know that savvy soldiers rested when and where they could.

"A penny for your thoughts," he said.

"You wouldn't get your money's worth."

"That bad?"

"Not bad, exactly," she replied. "Just...never mind."

"We've got the best part of an hour yet to go, if nothing else happens. Feel free to share whatever's on your mind. Or not. Your call."

She half-turned in her seat and said, "I thought I'd put this part of it behind me. It was in the rearview, right? Sure, I'm *involved* at Langley and directing things, but getting out here in the trenches or whatever, that's supposed to be a youngster's job."

"You still look good to me. Youngish, I mean."

"Right. Thanks for that, I think. But losing Roland was a shock, you know? I mean, you never met him, but he was...a decent guy."

"No doubt."

"I mean, we weren't...you know..."

"It never crossed my mind," Jack said.

"Which brings me to the barn."

Oh, God. The talk.

"Sara—"

"Just let me get it out, okay?"

Cody responded with a nod.

"I had a good time, Jack. I mean, a *great* time, but...well..."

"Let me stop you there. I wasn't making more of it than what it was."

"Oh. Right. Well, good."

"Because we've worked together, and we will again, presumably. That is, if we get through tonight alive."

"You're such a charmer."

"I get that a lot. But seriously, Sara, have no fear. I'm not the stalking type, unless it's part of an assignment."

When she laughed at that, it sounded honest. "So, we're good then?"

"Good as gold."

"I hope so," she replied. "Because I'm running out of friends."

"There's always Boyd," Jack said.

"We get along okay, most times, as long as I remember who he's really working for."

Cody feigned shock. "You mean, it's not strictly the USA?"

"As if. I'm talking first and foremost here. He serves The Man, and that's a gig of limited duration unless he can build a rep that carries on."

"You're sounding cynical these days."

"I think of it as realistic. Should we just agree to disagree?"

"I think we're on the same page, Sara," he replied.

"If we can just make it to Tashkent..."

"Right. I'm working on it."

Sara glanced across at him and said, "It isn't you that worries me."

Tashkent, Uzbekistan

Roberto Esperanza—"Bob" to all his white-bread buddies—wasn't thrilled at being low man on the Diplomatic Service totem pole, particularly when it landed him in boiling water.

Like today.

The U.S. Embassy in Tashkent stands at No. 3 Moy-qorghon Street, Fifth Block, in the Uzbek capital's Yunusobod District, north of downtown. Crowded with schools, bazaars, tennis courts and videogame arcades, plus one mediocre shopping mall, the district was named for Bolshevik hero Sergey Kirov—murdered by ex-friend Joseph Stalin's men in 1934—but was renamed in 1991, when the Soviet Union dissolved. Reaching the embassy from the nearest subway station, Khabib Abdullayev, requires a five-minute car ride or a walk clocked at twenty-five minutes.

Living inside the compound proper spared Bob Esper-anza that, along with daily hassles on the streets in general. State Department travel advisories cautioned tourists against potential terrorist attacks and "localized civil disturbances" sparked by various Islamic terrorist groups, but the worst threat so far during 2019 was a measles outbreak noted in late February.

Still, it was best to stay inside embassy walls and buttoned down.

Arranging what had been demanded by the U.S. Presi-dent—via some aide he'd never heard of previously, Denham Boyd—was turning out to have some wrinkles in it. First, Bob had confirmed Boyd's name and White House post, ensuring that some wily bastard wasn't punking him, then he had gone to work at hyper speed.

The main problem was working around the Uzbek establishment, more specifically the Ministry of Internal Affairs and its National Security Service, abbreviated "SNB" from Russian, described by Amnesty International as an oppressive "secret police force". Where local law enforcement was concerned, not much seemed to get done, a fact reminding Esperanza that the Ministry's acronym—MIA—could also stand for "missing in action".

His problem now...well, one of them...was that the SNB controlled Uzbekistan's Frontier Service, aka the National Border Guard. Its well-armed agents scrutinized all travelers entering or leaving the country, detaining those who sparked suspicion, allegedly torturing some and making other disappear entirely.

Foreign Minister Abdulaziz Khafizovich Kamilov made half-hearted efforts to tamp down bad publicity if he was in the mood, while walking a tightrope between Uzbek President Shavkat Mirziyoyev and the United States. America had recognized the Uzbek government in 1992, then saw relations take a nosedive after 9/11 and the Afghan invasion. Things had mellowed out a bit between the nations over the past dozen years, and Uzbekistan had quit the Russian-led Collective Security Treaty Organization—Moscow's answer to NATO— in 2012, but it wouldn't take much to set sparks flying again.

A bloody border incident, for example.

Bob didn't have a clue what U.S. agents had been doing lately in Afghanistan, nor did he care to know. His brief, now, was to help two of those agents get across the border in one piece and stash them at the embassy until their transport home could be finessed.

And in the process—thanks for nothing, Denham Boyd—he had to help them stay alive.

And when in doubt, ask the U.S. Marines.

Kunduz Province

Sara Durell regretted bringing up their heat-of-crisis interlude with Jack, but it was done now and behind them. Or at least she hoped it was.

They had enough to think about in terms of physical survival on the road, without allowing personal emotions to intrude. The Husky TSV's odometer claimed they were forty-odd miles from the Uzbek border now and making fairly decent time, considering the trackless desert they were crossing. Thirty miles per hour felt like a snail's pace on a freeway in the States—call it a traffic jam—but in the wild lands of Afghanistan it wasn't bad.

She kept her AK carbine cradled in her lap as if it were a child, but this "kid" crafted out of steel and wood never woke up with colic in the middle of the night, or bawled for food, much less to have its diaper changed. Switch out an empty magazine and you were good to go.

With luck, she wouldn't have to use the piece again on this mission, but luck—the good kind—seemed to be in short supply these days.

Whatever waited for them down the road—more Talib

fighters, Afghan regulars, or Uzbek border guards—she and Cody would take them as they came. Allowing for the worst scenario, a firefight on the misnamed Friendship Bridge itself, Sara intended to do anything and everything she could to stay alive and keep Cody that way as well.

So far, she had Denham Boyd's assurance of "help" with the border crossing, whatever that meant. The gap between Washington "help" and real-world relief was often a yawning chasm—witness Puerto Rico after Hurricane Maria back in 2017, or New Orleans after Hurricane Katrina twelve years earlier. She had no doubt Boyd would reach out to someone at the Tashkent embassy, but where it went from there was strictly up for grabs.

Tashkent was 6,300 miles from D.C., a whole other world in more ways than one. Formerly a satrapy of Moscow, Uzbekistan now billed itself as a "unitary presidential constitutional republic", but most observers ranked it as an authoritarian state on par with East Germany during the Cold War, with communism swapped out for Islam. Deputy Chief of Mission Alan Meltzer ran the embassy these days, pending Senate confirmation of ambassadorial nominee Daniel Rosenlbum as Tashkent's new ambassador, and rocking boats was definitely not on anybody's to-do list while staffers at the embassy marked time.

Still, Sara clung to faith that *something* could be done. And if that faith turned out to be misplaced...well, she would deal with that eventuality when it occurred.

That would be bad for all concerned, but Sara wouldn't have to sweat it.

If that came to pass, the living would be stuck with any mess she left behind.

Baghlan Province

"You have information for me?" asked Sediq Qayoumi.

"Yes, sir." The smile on Ehsan Abarkhyl's face was so unexpected, so unusual, that Qayoumi found it a bit disturbing, as if a psychopath was striving to convey emotion without feeling it.

"Well?"

"We've got photos from a drone in Kunduz Province, sir. A Husky TSV resembling one that's missing from the last engagement."

"When you say 'resembling'…"

"They all look the same, sir, but ours are repainted after liberation from the Brit Crusaders and they have no markings to identify them."

"While the NATO vehicles have coded numbers on their roofs or bonnets, to enable tracking from the air."

"Precisely, sir."

"How confident are you that this is the right TSV, Ehsan?"

"Given the time and place, sir, it is virtually certain."

"Virtually," Sediq echoed his subordinate. "I've never liked that word. It leaves too much to chance, don't you agree?"

"I do, sir. But considering the circumstances we cannot allow it to proceed unchallenged."

"True enough. Who stands between this so-called Husky and the Uzbek border now?"

"A Red Unit under the command of one Latif Hosseini. He seems competent enough."

"And he would not have been promoted otherwise."

"No, sir."

"But remind me. Omar Jamalzadah and Sandjar Zadran were both deemed competent as well, weren't they?"

"Yes, sir."

"And where are they tonight?"

"Both dead, sir."

"Dead, with all their soldiers. A significant depletion of our ranks."

"Latif assures me that he will not let the fugitives escape."

"I hope he's right, Ehsan. For all our sakes."

"Sir, should we share this information with Captain Isani?"

Pausing to consider that, Sediq Qayoumi frowned, then caught himself at it and tried to keep his face deadpan. "We could, Ehsan...but why disturb him prematurely, when we have no solid information to impart?" Still smarting from the Pakistani's insults, he added, "Better, I think to give him the confirmed results when we have been successful, eh?"

Abarkhyl's thin, unsettling smile returned as he replied, "My thoughts exactly, sir."

"Good. It's agreed, then. Stop and clear the vehicle, then bring our faithful ally up to date."

Would Ehsan read the not-so-subtle mockery in Sediq's tone? What if he did? Qayoumi personally thought it was high time the Taliban got by without kissing some Pakistani politician's ass.

Hibatullah Akhundzada, leader of the Taliban at large and presently a fugitive from the Crusaders, hiding out in Pakistan's Balochistan Province, might well disagree, but what of it? No man lived forever, and revolutionary leaders had a higher death rate than most. Assassins had nearly killed Akhundzada at Quetta, in 2012, and an American drone had slain Akhundzada's predecessor in May of 2016.

Men died in war, and Akhundzada, at fifty-eight, had already lived longer than most.

With any luck at all, Fate might step in to aid Sediq Qayoumi's prospects for promotion through the ranks. And when that happened, Pakistan might just be in for a surprise.

"A drone contact, you say?" Captain Isani asked.

Ali-Shir Samadzai, an informer whom Isani had recruited from the Taliban for two hundred rupees per month—the equivalent of $1.40 U.S.—bobbed his slightly misshapen head in agreement.

"Yes, sir," he replied. "A vehicle believed stolen this very night by two Crusaders in Kunduz Province. A Red Unit is closing in to trap them now."

Isani would not tell his spy that this was news to him—surprising news, in fact, since Sediq Qayoumi had pledged to keep him updated on any crucial information from the chase. And what could be more crucial than impending apprehension of the fugitives?

Isani wondered if he'd gone too far in threatening to sever ISI's connection with the Taliban. In fact, he did not hold that power and it was unlikely that he could persuade Director General Asim Munir to cut those ties, risking a blockage in the flow of information coming from Afghanistan to his headquarters in Islamabad.

Perhaps there was another way around the problem, getting rid of Sediq Qayoumi and filling his post with another more cooperative Talib. Accidents could be arranged. A bit of information passed along anonymously to some aide for Marine Corps General Kenneth McKenzie, commander of the United States Central Command, a part of "Operation Freedom's Sentinel", attached to NATO's "Operation Inherent Resolve".

"Resolve," Isani had discovered, seemed to be an English synonym for imperialism, decoded as, "We've got your country now and we ain't going anywhere."

Crusaders. How Isani wished and prayed the very earth would open up and swallow all of them alive.

Meanwhile, since that did not appear likely, he might just use USCENTCOM to solve a problem of his own, by sending his duplicitous "brother" Sediq Qayoumi to *Jahannam*, courtesy of a drone-dispatched Hellfire missile.

What could be more appropriate? An aptly named vehicle eliminating one who had attempted to deceive Isani by concealing information gathered from a drone.

"I thank you for this information," said Isani. "It is much appreciated."

"And my pleasure, Captain. All in service to the Allah's holy jihad."

"Of course. *As-Salaam-Alaikum*, my friend."

"*Wa-Alaikum-Salaam,* Captain, sir."

As a token of his gratitude, Isani gave Ali-Shir Samadzai a ten-rupee note and watched the peasant warrior smile.

It might, he thought, turn out to be the best seventy cents he'd ever spent.

Kunduz Province

Latif Hosseini braced one hand against the dashboard of his Jeep staff car, clutching his AK-74 by its barrel with his free hand while the weapon stood upright between his knees.

He wished the jolting ride was over and they could confront their enemies at last. Hosseini's driver, Qais Wafa, pushed the Jeep as if he were competing in a European Grand Prix race, without regard to Hosseini's comfort as they barreled over rough, dry land. Latif imagined that their pace was perilous, but they had no spare time to waste.

If he could not locate the enemy in time, Hosseini knew he might as well be dead, regardless of the cause.

It seemed to him a change was brewing in the Taliban, although he could not put his finger on the how or why of it. Some members of his Red Unit—albeit quietly, discreetly—had expressed dissatisfaction with the role of Pakistani agents in the movement. Granted, both Afghanistan and Pakistan officially declared themselves "Islamic Republics", but there were gaping rifts even within the One True Faith.

Afghanistan's last census showed its population to be 99.7 percent Muslin, whereas Pakistan claimed only 96 percent, the rest including Hindus and Christians. Beyond that commonality, 90 percent of Afghan Muslims followed Sunni Islam, only 7 percent being Shiites. Pakistan's division was greater, only 75 percent Sunni versus 20 percent Shiite, the rest describing themselves in polls as "just Muslims".

Scandalous!

The worst part, though, had been Pakistan's waffling support for the Taliban. Had not Pakistani's elected a radical female as prime minister before true believers came to their senses and assassinated her in 2007? On the other hand, Islamabad's warplanes had bombed Shia strongholds of anti-Taliban resistance, causing a rift with mostly-Shiite Iran—yet another "Islamic Republic"—while touching off a proxy war between Teheran and Sunni Saudi Arabia, waged on Pakistani soil.

Someday, Latif was confident, that conflict in the faith would be resolved, even if it required intervention by Allah Himself. In the meantime, however, the Taliban accepted military aid from Pakistan while striving to maintain its own identity, a contradiction that had strained relationships between the nations to a breaking point.

Tonight, with any luck, Latif Hosseini would bring glory to the cause by capturing the two Crusader fugitives who had embarrassed and destroyed two other Red Units within as many days. At one bold stroke, he could enhance the Talib movement and, if only incidentally, advance himself within it.

Pride is a cardinal sin in Islam, as in Christianity, but chiefly as it led proud men into rebellion against God. And if Hosseini's pride was simply pleasure in his service to Allah, how could it weigh against him in the end?

Indeed, what honored leader of jihad had ever been a truly humble man, whatever he espoused in private life? A certain kind of person—charismatic, bold and ruthless—was required to lead the masses in their war against apostasy.

Why not Latif Hosseini?

As the desert passed him, arid miles devoured by his convoy's headlights, he could think of no good reason in the world.

Unless, perhaps, he botched the move and wound up dead.

Jack Cody flicked another glance at the Husky's odometer, the dashboard lights somewhat distorted through his AN/AVS-6 night-vision goggles, pleased that they had covered nine more miles without a mishap to their captured vehicle.

Progress, but still at what felt like a creeping pace. He couldn't shake the knowledge that pursuers were somewhere behind them, bent on catching up and finishing the game. As far as what lay waiting for them up ahead...

The final border crossing worried him, always assuming they could ever reach that point. There had been no word back from Washington, which Sara seemed to take as normal, but the silence chafed at Cody's nerves, etching a blood-red question mark over their future.

If they made it to the border, if her guy in Washington had managed to arrange a helping hand across the Friendship Bridge, they had a chance. But in the murky world of Middle Eastern politics, entangled with religion constantly at war within itself, Jack knew they couldn't count on anything.

Nothing, that is, except more strife.

"You think they're waiting for us," Sara said, surprising him.

"How long have you been reading minds?"

"It's what I'd do, if the positions were reversed," she said. "Have someone up ahead, more coming up behind. Your classic pincer movement."

"Maybe we got ahead of them, after the last run-in."

"You don't believe that, though, do you?"

"I'd give long odds against it," Jack agreed.

"That's if you were a betting man."

"It's never been my thing."

"Too much like having fun?" she teased.

"Too much like flushing money down the crapper."

She shifted gears again. "So, if and when we meet them…"

"Call it 'when'."

"You have a plan?"

"The same as yours, I'd guess. Get through it. Stay alive and see what happens next."

"Some life," she said.

"Until we get a better one." He heard the way that sounded,

starting to correct it. "Hey, I didn't mean—"

"I know that," Sara cut short his apology.

"Okay."

They rode in silence for another mile or so, Jack wondering if he had stepped into a mine field unintentionally. Since his family was stolen from him, he had shied away from anything that felt like positive emotion, focused on the rage that kept him moving forward, constantly in search of enemies to vanquish and eradicate.

Why not? What else remained for him except the hunt—and at its end, the kill?

And speaking of the end...

"Jack?"

"Yeah," he said. "I see them."

Headlights boring through the darkness, southbound, hard on a collision course. Before long, they would blind him, glaring through his goggles, so Jack took them off and grabbed his, slapped it on and fastened its chin strap.

"I would have taken you for a fedora man, if you were into hats."

"Sorry to disappoint you."

"Do you plan on crashing?"

"Plan?" He almost laughed aloud. "I'd say that's stretching it."

"So, just hang on and make the best of it?"

"What else?"

"Okay. I guess I'll see you on the other side."

Or not, Jack thought, but kept it to himself.

CHAPTER 13

Ten pairs of headlights. No, make that eleven, as a smaller vehicle swung out from eating dust behind what Cody took to be an APC of some kind.

How many armed opponents crowded into those approaching Jeeps, trucks, and whatever? Cody didn't have a clue, and there was no point wasting time on hypotheticals.

If he and Sara hoped to see another sunrise, it was time for Jack to get his ass in gear.

"Hang on," he cautioned Sara, ready with her AK carbine in the stolen Husky's shotgun seat.

"I'm ready," she advised him.

Jack reached down with his left hand and switched the Husky's headlights on, an open challenge to the Taliban commandos fanning out across his path. He knew they were committed to their mission, even unto death, but now Jack wondered just how eager any given member of the team might be to die.

Fighting, okay. He had no doubt of that, although a couple of insurgents had tried running out on last night's free-for-all. But would their driver's risk a head-on crash and fiery death to stop their enemies?

There was no time for flipping coins now, even if Jack could have spared a hand to fish around inside his pockets for a stray afghani. He had their Husky TSV charging on a collision course with what he took to be another Taliban Red Unit, still miles from their goal of exiting Afghanistan.

The good news: whether they got through or not, Sara had passed on her intelligence and spurred a swift reaction from the U.S. Navy's Fifth Fleet, headquartered in the island Kingdom of Bahrain. Whether or not its cruise missiles had wiped out every trace of Devil's Rain—Jack knew damned well the rockets hadn't put an end to Afghan opium and heroin—at least it was a start.

Maybe a wakeup call to Afghans who were sick and tired of being pushed around by Taliban fanatics for the past twenty-five years.

"Ready to light them up?" he asked Sara Durell, over the wind-rush nearly drowning out his words.

"As ready as I'll ever be," she answered, angling her little AKS-74U out through the open window on her side, prepared to fire left-handed.

"Okay. Let 'er rip!"

When she cut loose, Jack could hear the 5.45mm brass rattling across the Husky's roof, a foot or so above his head. Down range, his high-beams showed him FMJ rounds shattering the windshield on a Ford LTV, making its driver swerve into the path of an onrushing Humvee M1151. That impact slammed the Ford into a barrel roll and spoiled the Humvee turret gunner's aim, the tracers from his M2 Browning arcing off across the desert sky like random fireworks.

The Humvee tried to climb over the Ford pickup but couldn't pull it off. Meanwhile, one of the LTV's passengers bailed out and sprinted clear—almost, that is, before a Jeep clipped him and tossed him ass over teakettle, landing in a broken heap.

Not bad, all things considered, coming out of Sara's first short burst.

But other Talibs had the Husky's range now, more or less although their vehicles were jolting over rugged ground the same as Cody's, everybody's aim thrown off a bit. A bullet struck the Husky's windshield frame, an inch or less from cracking glass, and caromed off into the desert night. Jack ducked involuntarily, then caught himself at it and straightened in the driver's seat, holding his ripped-off ride rock steady on its ramming course.

Unless some of the Talib drivers flinched and veered away, he was about to get that entrée to oblivion he'd been pursuing since his wife and kids were massacred.

Taking Sara with him, though, which never figured in his dead-end plans.

Jack thought he owed her more than that, even ignoring what had passed between them recently, but worried that he'd passed the point of no return where any deviation from the path he'd picked became impossible.

And if they couldn't make it out, he'd be content to take as many of the crazed jihadists with him as he could.

Latif Hosseini had five seconds' warning via walkie-talkie, more or less before his enemies, approaching from the south, revealed themselves by switching on the captured Husky TSV's headlights. A few more seconds, then an automatic weapon opened fire upon his convoy from the stolen vehicle's passenger side and the ambush he'd planned began falling apart.

Dumb luck let the Crusader triggerman—or trigger *woman*—stitch a line of bullet holes across the windshield of a Ford LTV pickup truck the Taliban had liberated from its rightful ANA owners. Latif would never know whether the Ford's driver was killed outright, wounded, or simply blinded by a flying storm of pebbled safety glass. In any case, it had the same result.

Hosseini saw the LTV swerve out of line, even as his own driver veered off in the opposite direction to avoid incoming fire. A stunning *crash* echoed across the desert wasteland as their convoy's Humvee M1115 plowed into the pickup, flipped it through a tumbling roll, and flung one of its passengers into the path of Latif's swerving Jeep.

His driver cursed and tried to miss their flailing comrade on the fly but couldn't manage it. Impact rolled the unlucky Talib up across the Jeep's bonnet, his face striking the windshield on Hosseini's side and smearing it with blood before he fell away.

"*Souder oghala!*" Latif snapped, before regaining some of his composure. That had been Omar Ahrari, a relatively new recruit and young, but he would grow no older. Snuffed out at the age of twenty-two and on his way to *Jannah* now, according to the great, infallible *Quran*.

"Is he insane?"

The question came from Latif's wheelman, Zalmay Hazara, though clearly, he expected no reply. Rather than try to read the damned Crusader's mind, Hosseini snapped, "Give me a shot if you can manage it without destroying us!"

"Yes, sir!"

Hazara slowed the Jeep a bit, veering farther away from the oncoming Husky TSV, while Latif thrust his AK-107 through the open window on his side. The British vehicle came into frame, and he was just about to fire a burst of 5.45mm rounds when Zalmay hit a rut or pothole on the sandy ground and spoiled Hosseini's aim.

"*Kona ke de mandam!*"

"Sorry, sir!"

"Watch what you're doing, damn it! Now I've lost them!"

But the enemy had not lost him. A three- or four-round burst from the Husky's passenger side drilled holes across Hosseini's door, one drilling through to trace a line of fire across his thighs and force a gasp of pained surprise between clenched teeth.

Hosseini fought the urge to spew more blasphemy, instead

managing two quick shots as his intended targets swept past him, northbound, aware that both had missed their mark. Around him, other Talibs filled the desert night with muzzle flashes, flying slugs, at least one of them striking Latif's Jeep by accident.

He cursed again and snatched the walkie-talkie from his staff car's cup holder, keying the "SEND" button and shouting to his troops, "Be careful where you're aiming, idiots! They're past us now. Get after them!"

And to his cringing driver, then, "Zalmay! Turn back! If they escape, we're all dead men!"

Baghlan Province

"Latif Hosseini's unit has made contact," said Ehsan Abarkhyl.

"And?"

Sediq Qayoumi knew there must be more. As an American might say, he waited for the other shoe to drop, expecting that from the look on Ehsan's face that it must be bad news.

"They're in pursuit, sir."

"In pursuit?" The words seemed to taste bitter, like a sip of rancid goat's milk. "Explain, Ehsan. Hosseini was supposed to intercept and stop them."

"Yes, sir. I only spoke with his *lomri baridman*—"

"His lieutenant?" Sediq interrupted. "Who is that?"

"Ishaq Tarzi."

"Ah, yes. Presumably Latif himself could not be bothered to report?"

"Tarzi reported they were under fire, sir."

"Under fire?" Qayoumi grimaced, felt his blood pressure spiking. "Another Red Unit unable to eliminate two enemies? Now *they* are 'under fire'?"

"Sir—"

"What else did this person say, Ehsan?"

"That they have taken casualties but are in pursuit."

"Merciful Allah! *In pursuit?*" Qayoumi fairly spat the bitter words. "Which means the damned Crusaders have escaped from them and are proceeding to the border?"

"Ishaq Tarzi says two of their vehicles have been disabled, sir. He offered no details. Our conversation was cut short, but I could hear gunfire."

"We are surrounded by incompetents, Ehsan. I should have gone to set the final trap myself."

To that, his aide made no reply. Fuming, Sediq demanded of Ehsan, "Where are they now, this minute?"

"It is difficult to say, sir. Once the enemy slipped past them—"

"Merciful Allah! Slipped past them?"

"Please remember, sir, these same Crusaders have destroyed two other Red Units so far."

"And you think I've forgotten that, Ehsan? Am I an idiot, like our commanders in the field?"

"No, sir. But—"

"Silence! Where is this fiasco presently occurring?"

"In Kunduz Province, as you know, sir. I would estimate some thirty-odd miles from the Uzbek border."

"And I take it that we cannot reach the site in time to make a difference?"

"Without air transport, no sir. Also, with the battle still ongoing and in motion..."

"Yes, yes. It appears that we are helpless, eh? Are you aware of what that means, Ehsan? What happens to us if the spies escape?"

"As to specifics, sir—"

"Stop! I shall clarify it for you, so that there is no misunderstanding. If we fail to stop them on our own ground, consequences shall result. There is no reason to believe we will survive them."

"But—"

"How long until they reach the border at their present rate of travel?"

"I have no idea, sir."

"'No idea, sir'," Sediq, scowling, mocked his aide.

"Ishaq Tarzi did not mention a specific speed of travel, sir, but with some nine or ten vehicles in pursuit of one—"

"And what word from our so-called friendly captain from the ISI?"

"Nothing, as yet, sir. I've obeyed your order not to contact him."

"Thank Allah for small favors. Do we have another unit in the area that might assist Hosseini?"

"Not that I'm aware of, sir."

Sediq Qayoumi felt as if his head was going to explode. "Well, *make* yourself aware! Get on the radio! Find out!"

"Yes, sir!"

"And failing that, Ehsan, you might be wise to pack your bags."

Kunduz Province

"You seeing this?" Sara Durell asked Jack.

"It's hard to miss," Cody replied.

The nine remaining Talib vehicles were turning to pursue them, raising clouds of dust illuminated and turned ghostly by their overlapping headlights. No one stopped to pick up passengers from the disabled Humvee M1115, leaving them behind and shouting after their distracted comrades, choking in the storm of flying grit.

Nine vehicles, some of their occupants already firing as they rolled out in pursuit of Jack and Sara in the Husky TSV they had appropriated from the last Red Unit they'd annihilated, others waiting while their frenzied drivers swerved around, trying to head off any more collisions.

"Numbers?" Sara asked him, facing backward from her seat.

"I'd have to guess," Jack said. "The better part of thirty, anyhow."

"That's what I was afraid of," she replied.

As she was watching, two of their pursuers had a fender-bender but both vehicles recovered, separated without difficulty, and resumed the chase.

"Determined little bastards," she remarked.

"They have to figure it's their last chance," Jack replied.

"And ours, too."

"We could stop and face them."

"You mean circle up the wagons?"

"Right. Except we've only got one wagon."

"Not the best idea you've had all day."

"Have to outrun them, then."

She glanced back at the dash, specifically the Husky's fuel gauge, with the needle indicating roughly half a tank of gas.

"At least we won't run dry."

"Least of our problems," Cody said. "We need to thin the herd."

"I could try shooting from the turret," she suggested.

"Might as well," he said. "You'd better take my piece, though. The bandoleer of 40mm rounds is down between our seats."

"Got it," Sara replied, laying her small carbine aside as she retrieved Jack's AK-107 with its GP-25 grenade launcher and the remaining cannisters to feed it. "Sure you don't mind someone messing with your weapon?"

Cody barked a laugh at that. "Not like it matters now."

"No, I guess not."

Taking his hardware with her, Sara scrambled from her seat up front and stood hunched underneath the Husky's turret hatch. A simple twist released it and she pushed it open, checking to be sure the *Kostyor* launcher had a round in place before she shrugged into the bandoleer.

With the top hatch open, all the firing from behind them suddenly grew louder. Sara pictured rising through the turret and immediately dropping backward, with a bullet in her brain. It was a calculated risk, but they were swiftly running out of time.

"Hold steady if you can," she cautioned Jack.

"I'll do my best."

"Same here."

Exposed, she felt the wind rushing around her, whipping hair about her face. Too late to tie it back now, with her hands full, muzzle flashes winking at her from the vehicles rolling in hot pursuit. Their bullets whining around her like a swarm of hornets, furious at a disturbance of their nest.

Aiming, she muttered to herself, "All right, you assholes. Come and get it."

Baghlan Province

Captain Isani barged into Sediq Qayoumi's headquarters, brushed past his aide without a by-your-leave, and moved to stand before Qayoumi's cluttered desk. The Taliban commander rose to face him, the expression on his face denoting consternation.

"We were not expecting you, Captain," Qayoumi said.

"Clearly, since you have chosen to deceive me. But as you can see, I've found out nonetheless."

"Found out precisely what?"

"Don't play the injured innocent with me, Sediq. You know damned well what I'm referring to."

"The fugitives," Qayoumi said, not asking him.

"None other."

"There was no time to alert you," lied Sediq, "but it was on my list of things to do."

"Tomorrow, possibly? The next day? Maybe when you'd had a chance to run and hide somewhere?"

"Mohammed, you forget yourself." No honorific "Captain" now.

"Do I?"

"Indeed. First, you appear to think that you are still in Pakistan, where you command allegiance, and that I am one of your subordinates. In fact, neither is true."

"You may wish to consult Commander Akhundzada about that."

"I think not. Just because your people shelter him in Pakistan, it does not mean you rule over the Taliban."

"We've had this talk before, Sediq."

"But failed to reach a resolution, it would seem."

"I stand to lose as much as you do if the fugitives escape."

"Hardly," Qayoumi said. "We both know that you'll blame it all on me, and if you suffer any consequence at all, it may be reassignment. On the other hand, failure means death to me."

"The risk of any warrior."

"Complicated by demands to let you meddle in affairs that don't concern you."

"This grows tiresome, Sediq."

"Feel free to leave, Mohammed. You may leave my office and Afghanistan, for all I care."

"Is this a dead man speaking to me?"

"No. A field commander trying to survive and carry out his orders from the one to whom he's sworn allegiance."

"All I wish to know, Sediq, is what you're doing to control the situation."

"Everything within my power. It demands my full attention, meaning that I have no further time to waste on you."

"You've lost two of your Red Units already, yes? And now you have a third at risk."

"You speak as if the choice was yours and you are in command."

Isani answered back, "And *you* behave as if your guns and money grow on trees, the way your poppies sprout out of the soil—or did, before your lax security allowed intruders to collect intelligence from your headquarters and initiate missile attacks."

Qayoumi scowled at him, asking, "Have you some purpose in appearing here without an invitation, other than to waste my time with insults?"

"You may find this difficult to grasp, Sediq, but I had hoped to save you from yourself."

"Such generous beneficence! And how would you do that, pray tell?"

"By offering timely assistance, if you have the common sense required to take it."

Sediq eyed Isani as he might a viper or a scorpion, then

sighed and sat back down behind his desk. "All right, then, for the sake of argument," he said. "Explain."

Kunduz Province

"Faster!" Ishaq Tarzi snapped at Youssof Gula, driver of his M939 series five-ton 6x6 truck made by AM General in the United States, appropriated from Camp Leatherneck U.S. Marine Corps base in Helmand Province seven months ago.

"Yes, sir! I'm trying, sir!" Gula replied through gritted teeth.

"Try harder, then, before they get away!"

Tarzi knew the truck's basic mechanics, powered by a Cummins NHC-250 engine generating 240 horsepower, with a five-speed automatic transmission. It weighed the better part of twelve tons, not counting the fourteen troops in back, with their assorted weapons. A top speed of sixty-three miles per hour left it outclassed by enemy Husky's seventy mph, not to mention their own convoy's lighter vehicles, and Tarzi raged at the constraints of his machine, watching the firefight slowly pull away from him with taillights screened by dust, and growing smaller by the moment.

"By Allah's beard, I could jump out and run faster than this?" Tarzi complained.

Gula could have disputed that, remarked on the absurdity of Tarzi's words, but that would only bring more insults down upon him, and perhaps provoke a slap across his sweating face.

Instead, the driver hunched forward, clutching the transport's steering wheel, pressing its gas pedal until the steel floor plate arrested further movement.

All in vain, it seemed.

Ahead of them, Tarzi could see the fleeing Husky with its female passenger partly exposed above the open turret, wind-whipped hair flying around her face, not covered by a modest scarf, much less a burka or the less modest hijab. She should have been an easy target in the glare of headlights following behind her vehicle, but no one had succeeded in disposing of her yet.

Instead, she braced a rifle—some sort of Kalashnikov, he saw—against her shoulder as a man would, triggering a hot round from the chunky grenade launcher mounted underneath its longer barrel. Tarzi could not hear the *pop* when it went off, but he could plainly see the puff of smoke before it blew away in tatters.

Now, a second later, he was nearly blinded by the flash of an explosion, as her high explosive round made impact on the bonnet of an ANA Toyota Hilux, shattering the pickup's front end like a giant hammer stroke, its driver and a front seat passenger propelled the windshield into a rising ball of fire.

Call it another four men dead, and still the damned Crusaders kept on rolling northward, seemingly impervious to harm.

Caught in a frenzy of frustration, Ishaq Tarzi cranked his window down and leaned outside, eyes narrowed down to slits against the flying dust and grit that churned up by faster vehicles in front of his. He grappled with his AKS-74, stock folder to reduce its length by ten inches, aiming as best he could without adjusting its iron sights. He had the rifle set for semi-automatic fire, conserving ammunition and reducing danger to his fellow freedom fighters who had outstripped his truck's progress.

Firing single shots, praying for guidance from Allah, he shouted after the fleeing Crusaders, "Die! Damn you, die!"

Sara Durell felt almost giddy from the mental rush of combat, fighting for her life and Jack's, knowing each second that she spent exposed above the Husky's gun turret might be her last.

It should have been intimidating, but she hadn't felt that way since she'd survived her first combat engagement years ago, when she had been a newly minted U.S. Army Green Beret, one of the first females to graduate from Special Forces training at Fort Benning in Georgia. She'd put up with a ton of shit to pull that off, survived it all, and earned respect the hard way on her first deployment to Iraq, with nine confirmed kills to her credit and a wounded comrade rescued under fire.

The rest was history, except the proving process seemed to endlessly repeat itself, next when she made the jump to Delta Force, and then to Langley with the CIA. The military and the government were still essentially boys' clubs, and sexual assaults on females in the service hadn't been eradicated yet—although one bum who'd tried it on with Sara spent the next six weeks in traction after "slipping on some stairs" and no one was the wiser but for certain servicewomen Sara had tipped off.

The would-be rapist had retired, unfit for anything but KP duty afterward, and Sara had kept track of him, updating local law enforcement as he moved from town to town. If he got tired enough of that...well, he could always take the nearest exit to the Other Side.

But now, with some two dozen Talibs vying to eliminate her, she was in her element. The first grenade she'd fired from Cody's 40mm launcher had destroyed a Japanese pickup the Talibs likely captured from some ANA contingent they had overrun, taking a few more fighters off the board.

It wasn't much, but not bad for a start.

Behind and down below her, at the Husky's wheel, Cody was holding it as steady as the landscape and their enemies allowed. The TSV was taking hits, of course, but nothing that had slowed it down so far.

The vehicles were manufactured with "variable level armor kits", ranging from none at all to heavy plating suitable for passing over certain land mines. None of them were indestructible, and hers was "lightly" armored, its protective cabin built of electrically welded high strength armor steel, the hull integrated with steel/composite modular add-on armor designed to repel small arms fire, grenade fragments, and lightweight improvised explosive devices.

All in all, it was a fairly stable ride, but not the fastest on the track by any means.

She fed another HE cannister into the Bonfire launcher,

but before unleashing it, picked up a Jeep knock-off approaching on the Husky's left-rear flank. A burst of 5.45mm rounds stitched spiderwebs across the almost-Jeep's windshield before it crumpled inward and the driver bought it in a splash of gore, slumping across the steering wheel. His shifting weight propelled the vehicle into a fishtail slid that turned into a stall and set him up for impact with a charging APC.

Before the driver of the larger vehicle recovered, Sara slammed her 40mm round into his grill and stopped the engine dead, smoke pouring out from underneath the hood, followed by yellow flames.

Her adversaries wouldn't get that fixed by triple-A.

And Sara found that she was laughing now, not so much in the face of Death, as at the crazy curves Life threw her way when she was least expecting it.

CHAPTER 14

Jack Cody would have called encouragement to Sara as she stopped another chase car in its tracks, a smudge of flame and smoke in the stolen vehicle's right-hand wing mirror, but he was focused on the road in front of him.

Or rather on the lack of one.

It would have helped to have a paved highway, but in the absence of such niceties, the Husky's LED dashboard array included with its standard features a directional compass and another gauging angles of climb or descent, as well as slopes to left or right while driving on uneven ground by day or night. He kept the compass needled pinned on due north, toward Uzbekistan, and otherwise just watched for any gullies, dry creek beds or sinkholes that would bring them to a screeching halt.

Which would, in turn, assure them of a swift and bloody death.

No great surprise or even disappointment there, for Jack.

But Sara, on the other hand…

His AK-107 stuttered from the Husky's turret once again, immediately followed by another *whomp* as Sara sent a 40mm round down range behind them toward their enemies. Jack checked his wing mirror again, in time to see an HE cannister explode under the front end of a pickup truck whose make he couldn't recognize amid the roiling clouds of dust.

No matter. Whatever the pickup's logo was, whoever made it piecemeal on some factory assembly line in the United States or Britain, maybe even Scandinavia, it was demolished in a microsecond, rearing on its back tires, grill and hood collapsing toward the windshield and the panicked faces screened by tinted safety glass. Its fuel line went up like a strip of detonating cord reaching the tank in nothing flat and setting off a fireball in the night.

Jack tore his eyes away, certain that anyone inside that flaming hulk was either dead or wishing that he was.

Fewer "insurgents" to confront if they were run to ground.

Jack loathed all terrorists, regardless of their race, their creed or nationality, but sometimes White House-speak confounded him. How could the same *mujahideen* be "freedom fighters" when the Russians barged into their homeland, welcoming assistance from the CIA, then be transformed into "insurgents" when Americans did likewise?

Granted, the U.S. was "justified" after the shock of 9/11, but its troops had missed Osama bin Laden and left him on the run for eight more years until another president sent Seal Team Six to run him down. Meanwhile, the wars spawned by two towers falling still dragged on, no end in sight, and seemed about to spread, encompassing the states of Syria and possibly Iran. Meanwhile, the Saudis who had planned and financed the original attacks were thanking Washington for new boatloads of weapons and an inside track to nuclear technology.

To hell with that, Jack thought.

No one had ever asked his views on U.S. policy, nor would they ever. At the moment, it was all that he could do, keeping himself and Sara breathing Afghan desert dust.

And those who meant to snuff them out were drawing closer all the time.

Latif Hosseini cursed again, and this time did not even bother asking Allah's pardon for his blasphemy. By his rough count, he had already lost about one-quarter of his fighting men and vehicles without inflicting any damage on his mortal enemies.

He snapped at Qais Wafa, urging him to greater speed, although Hosseini knew their Jeep—a Willys Overland CJ-3B—was at its limit now, straining to keep up with the Husky TSV stolen from Latif's murdered comrades by the two Crusaders he pursued. Vibrations rattling through the Jeep caused him to wonder how much longer it could keep pace with the motorized pursuit before it threw a rod or did whatever else a vintage vehicle might do in its death throes.

And if Hosseini fell behind the pack, let someone else collect the scalps he had been sent to claim, it likely meant the end for him as well.

So far, Hosseini had fired half a dozen shots at his intended victims, all in vain. As far as he could tell, none of his rounds had even touched the Husky TSV, much less its occupants. Meanwhile, the Yankee woman with her windblown hair had blasted three of his chase vehicles into oblivion, killing or gravely injuring the men inside.

How he would make her suffer if she fell into his hands, reminding her of what a female's place should be in battle and within the world at large.

Latif no longer thought in terms of *when* she would be captured. That had seemed inevitable when he led his full Red Unit south to meet the infiltrators, but it obviously was not working out as planned. The prospect of defeat, death and disgrace now loomed before Hosseini, and he understood what his compatriots—the other Red Unit commanders, dead now—must have felt during their last moments on Earth.

And none of it was good.

Baghlan Province

"Is that your plan?" Sediq Qayoumi challenged, making no attempt to mask his disappointment. "A last-minute ambush at the Uzbek border?"

"There is value in simplicity," Captain Isani said.

But not in simple-mindedness, Qayoumi thought. He kept that to himself and asked, as an alternative, "Do you have men in place?"

Isani nodded, lit another cigarette. Through rising smoke, he answered, "I prepared for this after your first Red Unit failed to stop the infidels. From here, I leave immediately for the front. There is a small airfield—"

"Outside of Puli Khumri," Sediq interrupted him. "We know it well."

Afghanistan boasted forty-five airports, large and small, all of them infiltrated by the Taliban. Puli Khumri, the capital of Baghlan Province, barely qualified, its airstrip capable of handling small helicopters and small planes the size of Piper Cubs or their equivalent, most owned by opium exporters operating under government protection.

"And upon arrival?" Sediq prodded the Pakistani agent. "What, then?"

"I have a team on standby from the Covert Action Division, veterans of the army's First Commando Battalion."

"The *Yaldrams*," Sediq said.

"None other. You are well informed...on that, at least."

Qayoumi would not let the Pakistani interloper bait him any further. "Well," he said, "since you are obviously in a hurry..."

Rising from his straight-backed chair, Isani said, "Believe me when I say, Sediq, I take no pleasure in preempting you. There is simply too much at stake. If you had solved the problem on your own..."

"Of course," Qayoumi said, remaining seated, making no attempt to shake Isani's hand. "You only want the best for all of us."

But mostly for yourself, he thought.

"I'm glad you understand. No doubt, we'll speak again when all of this unpleasantness is settled."

Not if I have anything to say about it, thought Sediq. But said, "Safe travels then. I wish you luck."

"*As-Salaam-Alaikum,* Captain."

"*Wa-Alaikum-Salaam,*" Sediq answered in his turn, by rote.

Isani left his office then, closing the door without a backward glance. Ehsan Abarkhyl entered seconds later, frowning as he asked Qayoumi, "Well, sir?"

"He is flying up to Kunduz Province, where he has an ambush prearranged."

"Should we have soldiers waiting to receive him?"

Sediq thought about it, then said, "No. If the Hosseini unit fails to stop our enemies, Isani's men may be our final chance." And then, after another moment's thought: "There will be time enough to deal with him at leisure, I suspect."

Tashkent, Uzbekistan

"So, are we clear on what's supposed to happen?"

As he spoke, Bob Esperanza frowned a little, hoping that he wouldn't get a hassle from the man in uniform who stood at ease across the desk from him, inside Bob's smallish office at the U.S. Embassy.

"Affirmative," his guest replied. "And this is duly authorized by the *chargé d'affaires,* sir?"

"As I said, Captain. It obviously won't be public knowledge, nothing for the media to spread around."

"No, sir. Just making sure this order is official, since we may be stepping on some tender toes."

"They'll heal. It may require a little sugar, but we're used to that."

"In that case, sir, we're good to go. I'll get my people set as soon as we're done here."

The speaker, Captain Lewis Butler, represented the U.S. Marine Corps Special Operations Command, commonly known in military-speak as "MARSOC". The marines assigned to it were amply trained for direct action, special reconnaissance and foreign internal defense, a range of activities broad and vague enough to cover damned near anything. With armed men backing him, Butler should just about be able to finesse the passage of two fugitives across the Friendship Bridge.

Or Esperanza hoped so, anyway.

But if it blew up in their faces, Bob knew he would be the one taking the fall. And it would be a long way down, without a safety net.

If it went sideways, Esperanza knew the order issued by the embassy's *chargé d'affaires* could disappear like magic, leaving him portrayed as a loose cannon operating on his own authority, unsanctioned by the State Department, by the Embassy, by anyone at all. Bob definitely couldn't count on Denham Boyd to pull his fat out of the fire from Washington, where White House aides were basically concerned with covering the boss's ass, then looking out for Number Two.

The answer to that problem: make damned sure the scheme came off as planned, without a hitch. Or anyway, without a hitch that nobody could sweep under the nearest handy rug.

And if Bob Esperanza couldn't pull that off, smart money said that he was in the wrong job anyway.

Kunduz Province

Sara Durell ducked under cover as a rifle bullet came too close for comfort, buzzing past her ear. She needed to reload Jack's AK-107, ditching its spent magazine and snapping in another from his bandoleer, taking the extra time to feed his *Kostyor* launcher with another 40mm round.

A thermobaric cannister this time, just for variety.

The XM1060 round used oxygen from the surrounding air to generate a high-temperature explosion, typically of longer duration than one produced by conventional condensed explosives. On a larger scale, it would have been a fuel-air bomb designed to immolate whole villages. The 40mm size was perfect for consuming vehicles and all their occupants.

"You good?" Jack asked her, from behind the Husky's steering wheel.

"So far," she answered back. "Just getting ready to surprise our friends."

Sara flexed her legs and poked her head above the level of

the Husky's turret, looking for another target in the dwindling line of vehicles pursuing them. She chose an M1117 Guardian ASV, limited to four people on board and armored against small arms fire, but still a rolling death trap if her thermobaric cannister struck home.

Aiming the *Kostyor* launcher with its notched quadrant sight, Sara fired from one hundred yards with the armored car advancing steadily, sending her round down range at some 250 feet per second. When it hit, a fireball overwhelmed the ASV, rolling from front to rear and sucking all the oxygen out of its passenger compartment, turning it into a four-wheeled oven. Although fitted with a gas particulate air filtration system to frustrate chemical attacks, nothing could save the Guardian's crewmen from roasting alive.

Hell of a way to go, she thought. *But if you aren't prepared for it, you had no business being in the game at all.*

Puli Khumri, Baghlan Province

The airport wasn't much to look at, just a bare dirt landing strip four hundred yards in length, beside a prefab building serving double duty as an air traffic control center of sorts and service area where a part-time mechanic worked on aircraft needing basic maintenance.

In case of major problems, pilots and their planes were out of luck.

Captain Isani's aircraft was a vintage Piper PA-44-180

Seminole, a twin-engine model debuted in 1979, with space on board for one pilot and three passengers. Its two Lycoming O-360-E1A6 air-cooled flat four counter rotating engines had a top speed of 193 miles per hour, with a range of 1,053 miles and a service ceiling of 17,000 feet. The plane was twenty-eight feet long, with a thirty-nine-foot wingspan, and weight of 2,354 pounds without cargo, tolerating a maximum takeoff weight of 3,800 pounds.

Captain Isani knew all that about the Seminole because he never trusted his life to any strange machine, without a microscopic understanding of its capabilities and limits. That held true from planes to earthbound vehicles, along with weapons ranging from handguns to field artillery.

He was a fighting man and proud of that, intent on clinging to his life at any cost.

Let young fools vie for martyrdom in Allah's name. Captain Isani meant to go the distance and emerge, if possible, unscathed at journey's end.

His pilot, and the Piper's only other occupant tonight, was Syed Nishtar, a Pakistan Air Force veteran of fifteen years who'd left the service as a second lieutenant when he joined the ISI's Covert Action Division, providing transport and such other services as were required. At sundry times that had included flying opium and heroin abroad, air-dropping weapons to the Taliban, and extricating ISI agents from foreign soil, occasionally under fire.

Isani could, and did, trust Nishtar with his life.

But he would leave him to their adversaries without

thinking twice, if he believed such treachery was justified.

Their destination was Kunduz Airport, located five miles south of the provincial capital and sixty-four miles north of Puli Khumri. A car stood waiting for Isani there, arranged by telephone after his issued orders for a Covert Action team to be on station at the Friendship Bridge spanning the Uzbek border with Afghanistan.

The team was small, four men, consisting of a dedicated marksman—or a "sniper," in the common parlance—with three backup soldiers packing automatic weapons for support. If they were fortunate, two long-range shots would finish off the white Crusaders who had cut a bloody swath through Sediq Qayoumi's unjustly celebrated Red Units, leaving dozens of bodies in their wake.

Two shots...and if that failed, the sniper's three support troops would stand ready with assault weapons to finish off the job, along with any border guards of hapless bystanders who crossed their lines of fire.

It would be yet another job well done where native forces failed, another feather in Isani's cap and, possibly, win him promotion to major, sporting a crescent and star upon his uniform's lapels.

That was an elevation he regarded personally as long overdue.

"Will there be action, sir?" Syed Nishtar asked when they were airborne, winging north.

Isani smiled and said, "I would not be at all surprised."

Kunduz Province

Ishaq Tarzi was spitting mad, nearly beside himself with rage. Nothing that he could do or say increased the M939 series truck's speed, falling behind the other vehicles remaining in the convoy as they trailed their quarry northward through the night.

Dawn would be breaking soon, and it might bring the Afghan Air Force down upon them, either A-29 Super Tucano pilots from the 81st Fighter Squadron with their 20mm canons and laser-guided 70mm air-to-ground missiles, or Mi-17 helicopter gunships from the Slovak Republic, with 3,300 pounds of "disposable stores" including bombs, gun pods and rockets.

That meant death for every Talib in the caravan who had not been annihilated yet, and Ishaq Tarzi, for his part, badly desired to live. As if that mattered to Allah, much less the field commander who had placed them in harm's way.

Granted, Tarzi had pledged his life to Allah's holy cause, but he was not particularly thrilled by the concept of guts without the glory, more particularly when said guts were his, scattered across the godforsaken desert's sand.

"Go faster, will you?" he urged Youssof Gula in the driver's seat.

"Yes, sir. I'm trying, sir," Gula replied.

And still the chase pulled out ahead of them, leaving them in its dust.

Sara felt a shudder through the Husky TSV, an altogether different feeling from the jolts and jostles she'd become accustomed to during their dash northward. She ducked down, raised her voice as she addressed Jack Cody, to be heard above the engine's noise and sounds of rushing wind.

"What's up?" she asked.

"We're overheating," he replied. "I haven't got a frigging clue what's going on."

"In other words, we're screwed?"

A *bang* from the TSV's engine punctuated her remark.

"I'd say you're right," Jack called to her. "We're running out of steam."

"And welcome to the freaking Alamo," she muttered to herself. And then, to Jack, "Toss me my carbine and I'll hand you back the 107."

"Never mind," Jack said, downshifting as the Husky rumbled to a sluggish halt. "You've done all right with it so far."

"Well, if you're sure..."

"Just keep a bullet in reserve."

"I heard that," she replied, and turned back toward the TSV's turret.

Nobody had to warn her about warding off live capture by the Taliban. Aside from their decapitation videos, she knew what female prisoners were normally subjected to by Allah's self-ordained commandos and she wasn't having it. She would be counting rounds from here on out, through Cody's AK-107 magazines down to her Glock, and when her moment came, she'd take the Kipling exit without thinking twice.

Like Jack, she had no family to leave behind her, grieving. Possibly a handful of acquaintances at Langley might slow down as they were passing by the Wall of Honor with her star among the rest, but memories were short in cloak-and-dagger work.

If this was the conclusion she'd been moving toward for years on end, subconsciously, at least she had been mentally prepared for it. And she would let the bastards know that they'd been in a fight.

Rising above the Husky's turret hatch, she signed with the Bonfire 40mm launcher, sent another HE round down range as her vehicle waddled to a halt, rewarded by a blast that sent men and machine parts tumbling across the desert floor. Reloading with another thermobaric round, she braced the rifle's butt against her shoulder, speaking softly to her enemies and to herself.

"Come on and get it, boys."

Latif Hosseini did not see the 40mm high explosive round hurtling to meet him, could not even glimpse the launcher's puff of smoke with all the dust and grit that roiled around his Jeep. But there was no mistaking impact when it happened: detonation ripping through the staff car from its grill on backward, shattering the windshield, blinding him with beads of glass.

The next thing that Hosseini knew, he was sprawled on the ground, the left leg of his trousers burning, hungry flames gnawing his flesh beneath the desert camo fabric. Screaming, he began to roll and thrash about, each movement driving spikes of agony into his pelvis and torso, trying to douse the fire.

His other pains, distinct and separate from scorching flesh, told Latif he was badly injured. Bones were broken, sharp ends gouging nerves inside, a splintered rib knifing one of his lungs. It seemed to take forever, putting out the fire, and even then, he wound up with a wracking cough, causing more jolts of misery inside his battered chest.

The stench of his own roasted flesh—or someone else's—triggered Latif's gag reflex. That nausea worsened as he remembered something that he'd read long years before, a doctor saying that whatever smells a human nose could register—burnt meat, dog shit, whatever it might be—consisted of small airborne particles from the offending source.

Hosseini smelled himself cooking, which meant he was inhaling microscopic fragments of his own seared flesh.

On balance, he would have preferred the dog shit anytime.

Gunfire echoed across the desert, while the sound of revving engines had subsided. When Hosseini tried to turn and make out what was happening, a new pain from his neck sent brightly colored spots dancing before his eyes.

All right.

At least the pain meant that he was not paralyzed. Dying, perhaps—yes, almost certainly—but he still had ability to move, albeit drastically restricted now.

If he could only find a weapon, crawl across the sand and with his last breath fire upon his enemies...

Latif had lost his rifle when the HE blast expelled him from his Jeep, but he still wore his holster with a Russian Makarov pistol inside it. After an eternity of fumbling with the holster's flap, he freed the handgun, did not bother cocking it because it seemed like too much work and he could simply squeeze its double-action trigger once an enemy was framed within its sights.

Hosseini started crawling toward the point where he could see his convoy's vehicles surrounding the Husky they had pursued for miles on end. The two Crusaders were not out of action yet, still fighting back and winnowing the Talib ranks. He simply had to creep across another twenty-five or thirty yards to join the fight.

And after that...

Perhaps he would awaken in *Jannah*.

Perhaps there would be nothing more for him at all.

Jack Cody carried Sara's AKS-74U carbine with him when he opened the driver's door on the disabled Husky, searching for targets. He flashed on *The Wild Bunch*, one of his all-time favorite films, and hoped he wouldn't fail Sam Peckinpah if this was all she wrote.

Up top, Sara was laying waste among the Talib warriors with his AK-107 and its *Kostyor* 40mm launcher, sowing brutal death among them with each trigger pull. Jack saw jihadists lurching, staggering and going down, blood spurting from their wounds, while battle smoke from burning vehicles and the eruption of grenades obscured the scene of carnage.

Cody waded into it, milking short bursts out of the stubby weapon in his hands. With three-round bursts it wasn't difficult to keep track of the carbine's load and know when it was time to swap out magazines. Jack simply had to duck incoming fire, leaving the TSV behind to dodge its ricochets and take the battle to his enemies.

Wet work deserving of its name.

The Afghan desert might be short on rain this season, but the blood that drenched its soil could cultivate a crop of death that was perennial.

Two turbaned jihadists were charging toward Jack through the haze of dust and battle smoke, firing wildly at they came. Unlike the shootouts filmed by Hollywood or Bollywood, pulling a trigger didn't guarantee a hit, much less a kill. Incoming rounds flew close enough for Jack to hear them sizzling past, but none had touched him yet, as he responded to the threat.

Two three-round bursts were all it took to end that threat, well placed at center mass, putting his human targets down. One dropped as if stone dead before he kissed the dirt, a final shiver passing through him as his lift took flight for parts unknowable. The other spun around and screamed, fell thrashing like a chicken recently decapitated, running out of steam and blood.

Another 40mm HE blast stung Cody's ears, its shockwave jarring him, and something like a hornet's sting lanced his right thigh. He reached down, fingers coming back blood-stained but not enough to indicate a major wound.

Shrapnel, whether from the grenade itself or scrap iron from whatever vehicle it had demolished, penetrating deep enough that he could feel it just below his epidermis, through the punctured fabric of his pants.

Another scar to carry with him on life's journey, if the trip wasn't concluded here and soon. Nothing that anyone he cared about would ever have a chance to see and question in a private moment.

Unless Sara...

As if summoned by his stray thought, her voice cut through Cody's fleeting reverie.

"Look out, Jack!"

He was turning in her general direction, eyes sweeping the battleground, when she squeezed off a single round from his Kalashnikov and Cody heard it strike something—some-one—in front of him, low down.

He found the Talib who'd been creeping up on him, worming his way along with knees and elbows, brandishing a dusty semiautomatic pistol. Sara's round had drilled into the dead guy's forehead, ending him before he had a chance to aim and fire at Jack.

And just like that, the noise of combat ended, tattered by a rising desert breeze that also cleared the field of floating dust.

Looking around, he spotted Sara moving toward him,

eyeing bodies on the hardpan as she passed them.

"Is that it?" he asked her, half afraid of jinxing it. "We done now?"

"Looks like it," she replied, risking a weary smile. "Our Husky's had it, though."

"No sweat," Jack said. "We've got more rides to choose from, if you haven't blown them all to Hell and gone."

CHAPTER 15

Kunduz Province

Sara had blown all the major fighting vehicles away with Jack's grenade launcher, which left them two rides they could choose from for the final journey north. One was a flatbed truck, deuce-and-a-half, too slow for Cody's taste. The other was a British Force Protection Ocelot, codenamed Foxhound, purchased to replace the older Snatch Land Rovers on desert patrols.

He felt at ease behind the Foxhound's wheel, night-vision glasses back in place—or, anyway, at ease within the limits of a ride that might turn out to be his last. Beside him, Sara still maintained a watchful attitude, but she was winding down from their encounter with the Taliban.

Resigned to whatever might happen next?

Jack wasn't sure, but he could not escape the snatch of golden oldie song that echoed through his brain.

Doris Day from the 1960s, before Jack was born, singing "Que Sera, Sera" from some movie whose title he couldn't remember, since once on late-night TV show.

Whatever will be will be.

Jack didn't buy that altogether, though he recognized there was a tide of human events that seemed to propel governments and their people through cycles of war and ceasefire, then more war. He couldn't say if stupid people simply failed to learn from history, or if their private bigotry and greed pushed them beyond the bounds of common sense.

"You think we'll make it?" Sara asked him, trying to sound casual.

"Best guess? I'd call it sixty-forty in our favor now. As for the Uzbek border guards...well, I don't have a clue."

"We can't shoot our way past them."

"No." That much, at least was obvious. "Maybe your buddy Boyd got lucky, pulling strings."

"I'd trust that more if we were headed for the Long Bridge over the Potomac," Sara answered.

"Roger that. You reckon he'll just leave us hanging?"

"Doubtful. That could lead to problems blowing back on State from Tashkent and the media. I think he'll *try* to help. But whether he can pull it off...well, I'm inclined to flip a coin."

And that was what Jack's life had come down to since terrorists had slain his wife and kids. A coin toss, knowing that a man who bets consistently against tall odds is bound to lose sometime, and likely sooner than later.

Maybe tonight?

"Just on the off chance, though," he said, and left it dangling there, unfinished.

"Then we do whatever we can manage on our own," Sara replied, "and take what comes."

"You've got my vote," Jack said, and offered her a smile that felt sincere—at least up to a point.

The Foxhound rumbled on, conveying Jack and Sara toward a meeting that might be their last, within sight of the Afghan-Uzbek Friendship Bridge.

Friendship with guards and guns, barbed wire and armored vehicles, that is.

Which Jack supposed was just about what passed for friendship in the modern, murky world of international relations.

Friendship Bridge, Termez, Uzbekistan

The Friendship Bridge seemed anything but friendly to Bob Esperanza in the first gray light of day. Its guards, Uzbek and Afghan, were on high alert since his arrival in a UH-60 Black Hawk chopper from the embassy, in company with Captain Lewis Butler and his well-armed MARSOC team.

Bob knew the Friendship Bridge's history. Ironically built in 1981-82 by Russian engineers, to keep their troops supplied while wreaking havoc in Afghanistan, in '89 it saw the final Soviets withdrawn, proclaiming victory while the "Free

World" proclaimed them losers on an epic scale. Uzbekistan had closed the bridge in 1997, when the Taliban was running wild across the river Amu Darya, finally reopening it in December 2001 as one of the most heavily guarded border crossings on Earth.

The present road and railway bridge, spanning 892 yards, would be hell to cross under fire. Make that impossible, unless the people seeking to traverse it were prepared to mount a determined assault against ardent defenders with reinforcements on tap. Esperanza had done what he could, working through the Tashkent embassy's *chargé d'affaires* to finesse cooperation from the Uzbek Ministries of Internal Affairs, but those departments were often at odds with each other, both united in determination not to be perceived as America's lackey.

Call it a recipe for potential disaster, and if it all went south, Bob would be singled out for blame as the chef in question.

Termez lies 410 miles south of Tashkent by car, following the onetime Uzbekistan Silk Road, presently the Tashkent-Termez Highway. Bearing in mind that 15 percent of all Uzbek roads were unpaved, the remainder swiftly deteriorating from lack of proper maintenance, the drive averaged nine hours with "light" traffic, longer if a truck broke down or there was any kind of accident along the route.

Bob's team had cut that time by six hours and twenty-minutes, flying south in one of the embassy's UH-60 Black Hawk helicopters at 180 miles per hour overland, arriving to the consternation of border guards on the graveyard shift, forewarned by their commander but not mollified.

In broken English—make that "mutilated"—the night shift captain, sporting four gold stars and one blue stripe upon his tunic's epaulets, had tried to make it clear that he resented foreign interference with his job, but that he would obey the orders issued by his colonel, after consultation with the deputy director at the Committee for State Border Protection. He could not, of course, ensure that Afghan border guards would take the same approach.

"So, what about the Afghans," the Captain asked, as they retreated to their Black Hawk and his waiting MARSOC troops.

"I've cleared it through our embassy in Kabul," Bob replied. "Assuming anyone sent word up here, we ought to be all right."

"Terrific. Now, besides those 'maybes', all we have to think about are Taliban insurgents, maybe someone from the ISI on top of that."

"Sounds easy, when you put it that way," Esperanza said. "And in the immortal words of Jean Luc Picard, make it so."

"John Luke Who?" Butler asked.

Bob shook his head and answered, "Never mind."

Hariatan, Balkh Province, Afghanistan

Captain Mohammed Isani eyed the Friendship Bridge by dawn's first light, then turned to scan the bank of the Amu Darya, spotting the Covert Action Division troopers he'd assigned to watch and wait, assuming the Crusader fugitives escaped from contact with the Taliban.

And so they had.

Now it was up to him and to the special soldiers he'd hand-picked for this assignment, to prevent their enemies from making it across the river with their knowledge of conspiratorial events inside Afghanistan.

Isani's sniper would be taking point with his Accuracy International Arctic Warfare rifle manufactured in Portsmouth, England, a bolt-action weapon chambered for 7.62×51mm NATO rounds, equivalent to the venerable .308 Winchester. A skilled shooter could empty the rifle's ten-round detachable box magazine at a rate of one shot per two or three seconds, while the gun's Schmidt & Bender PM II telescopic sight with variable magnification granted pinpoint accuracy beyond one thousand yards.

Four to six seconds then, for Isani's man to eliminate both of his targets. With his bullets travelling more than a half-mile per second, outrunning sound, the sniper could drop both marks before bystanders heard the first shot's echo from across the Amu Darya.

He was looking forward to the show, but still had reservations. There was still no sign of the Crusaders, but a party of U.S. Marines had turned up on the far side of the Friendship Bridge by helicopter, accompanied and directed by a civilian whom Isani took to be some functionary from Tashkent U.S. Embassy.

That was good news and bad news, rolled up into one.

Clearly, Americans across the river were expecting company, and who else could that be except the fugitives Isani sought to silence? The marines, he though, were just for show. Standing on Uzbek soil, beside their Black Hawk, there was little—make that nothing—they could do to help a pair of targets on the Afghan side.

Nothing, that is, but wait and watch them die.

That prospect pleased Isani greatly. If he found it feasible, the captain hoped to watch the executions, then perhaps reveal himself to thumb his nose at the Great Satan based in Washington.

Isani reckoned that would make his day, perhaps even his year.

In fact, it might just be the crowning star of his career.

The Amu Darya River

Sniper Najmuddin Shahi kept watch on the south end of the Friendship Bridge through his rifle's telescopic sight, waiting for his intended targets to appear. The range, eight hundred yards, was well within his capability for reaching out to touch someone and end the designated victim's life within a second and a half.

The marksman had no photographs to help identify his targets. He knew both marks would be American, further assuming they were both Caucasian, since a black spy or Latino would stand out among Afghanis like the proverbial sore thumb.

He further knew that one of them was female, but that bothered him no more than any other killing task he'd been assigned while serving with the Pakistan Army or later, with the covert ISI. Shahi had killed women before—only a handful, granted, of his ninety-six confirmed kills in Yemen and Sri Lanka, North-West Pakistan and Saudi Arabia, along the Indian border, or hunting renegades for the Islamic Military Counter Terrorism Coalition.

He had never shot a child, so far, but thought that if it ever happened, accidentally or otherwise, it would not cost him any sleep.

As for a pair of damned Crusader spies, he cared no more about their lives than if they'd been a pair of cockroaches.

One he had fired—two shots, two kills, the usual result—protecting him would be a task for his support troops with their automatic weapons and grenades. Shahi did not imagine any Afghan border guards attempting to arrest or kill him, most particularly if he dropped his targets somewhere near the midpoint of the Friendship Bridge, in no-man's land.

Why should they even care?

But if he failed to carry out the task...well, that was something else entirely. Captain Mohammed Isani shared the unforgiving gene that military officers appeared to have in common, tolerating no failure by their subordinates. Shahi, a lowly *hawaldar* or sergeant in the ISI, would likely not survive bungling a mission of this magnitude, when all that it required of him was two clean shots.

Child's play.

When he was finished here, Shahi would only need another two kills to complete the magic hundred and, perhaps, retire. But was that what he really craved?

Was he prepared to leave behind the one thing that he'd ever truly loved?

The sniper drew back from his weapon's Schmidt & Bender telescopic sight to give his eye a fleeting rest. He did not have to watch the long bridge constantly. It should be fairly obvious when his targets approached, driving some kind of stolen military vehicle and jumping spaces in the waiting access queue to make their way across.

Or so they would expect.

But they'd be reckoning without Najmuddin Shahi and his trusty rifle standing by to drop them in their tracks.

That edge was all he needed in this misbegotten world.

Approaching Hairatan

"Where did you want to drop this off?" Sara Durell inquired.

Jack Cody had removed his black night-vision goggles as sunrise crept over the Amu Darya river, slowing into their half-mile approach to the imposing Friendship Bridge.

"I'm heading in as close as we can get," he answered, "then we'll leave the hardware in the vehicle and take a hike."

"And if there's no one here to meet us?"

"Then I guess that's all she wrote."

"You know, I've always wondered who the 'she' is, with her cryptic notes."

"I know that one," Jack said.

"Of course. you do."

"Well, do you want to hear it?"

"Go ahead, then."

"It's a punch line from a joke in World War II. Some GI gets a letter from his squeeze back home and starts to read it for his buddies. It begins, 'Dear John' and when they ask him to get on with it, he says, 'That's all she wrote.' Also, the first use of the 'Dear John' letter reference, more recently a song by rapper Eminem."

"Okay, then. Now, about our problem…"

"If we bail out lugging guns, the border guards won't let us pass. I doubt they'd even let us live."

"Damned if we do…"

"Or if we don't. You're catching on."

"Is this what it's been like for you, since coming over to the Company?"

"I can't complain," Jack said. "Truth is, I dropped the ball before I left the army. Got my ass kicked right out of the game."

"You're pretty active for a benchwarmer," she said.

"I have my moments."

"So I've noticed."

"Thank you, ma'am."

"And now I feel like someone's grandmother."

"You ever heard of Lepke Buchalter?"

"Some kind of old-time gangster, wasn't he?"

"The only big boss of the Syndicate who ever rode the lightning at Sing Sing."

"Is there a moral to this story?"

"Just a story," Jack replied. "One, while Lepke was purging witnesses against him, one of his cohorts came up and asked for money to ensure his silence. Lepke smiled and asked his age. The other guy said forty-something, and Buchalter told him, 'So, you've lived a nice full life'."

"Nasty."

"He made his point. A few more minutes and we'll go make ours."

"What happened to the other guy with Lepke?" Sara asked.

"He died."

"That's reassuring."

"Hey, it catches up with all of us."

"But I was hoping that it wouldn't be today."

"It hasn't yet," Jack said. "In fact, I think I see a place to park this rig right now."

The Friendship Bridge

Captain Lewis Butler pointed to the dusty armored vehicle approaching the Afghani side. "That must be them," he told Bob Esperanza.

"About freaking time," the man from State replied.

Just then, Staff Sergeant Emil Crabbe stepped up on Butler's left. "Captain, we've got a drone fix on four hostiles, half a mile upriver from the bridge."

Instead of pointing, Crabbe nodded his head and Butler

peered into the western distance, right around the river's nearest bend. He had a choice to make, whether to put his people back inside the Black Hawk for a sortie to the other side, or...

"Give me that radio," he ordered.

Sergeant Crabbe handed it over, ready to transmit. Butler identified himself, complete with service number, then ordered, "I want those bogeys taken out on my signal."

"Captain—"

"No arguments, Mister," he told the probable civilian sitting in a room without windows, several hundred—maybe thousand—miles away. "When I green-light it, drop the hammer on them or start filling out retirement papers. As for any pension, you can blow it out your barracks bag."

"Yes, sir! We're standing by."

He hung onto the two-way radio as their civilian watchdog, Esperanza, butted in.

"What's happening, Captain?" he asked.

"Four armed men standing by at sniping range," Butler replied. "I'm taking care of it."

Just then, a man and woman stepped out of the armored car, both looking shopworn, sneaking up on wasted. Spotting them, Bob Esperanza said, "They're ours, right there. We'd better get back in the chopper, eh?"

"I thought about it," Butler told him. "Ruled it out. We've got a better way to deal with opposition and provide a nice diversion all at the same time."

"Which is?"

"Eye in the sky," Butler replied. "And this one's got a sting-er, too."

"You don't mean—"

"Hell, I don't."

"But—"

"Mister Esperanza, if you haven't got the stomach for it, I suggest you take a stroll. I'll find you when we need you."

"Screw that, Captain. This got dumped in my lap and I'll see it through."

"Okay, then. You might want to warn the Uzbek border guards. We wouldn't want them getting hinky, taking out the friendlies."

"Right. Okay. I'll do that."

Esperanza headed over toward the Uzbek captain of the guard, trying to tell the local what was happening without gestures to give the game away for anyone who might be watching through binoculars or through a telescopic rifle sight.

At this point, Captain Butler wouldn't mind if his opponents cut and ran. He definitely *would* mind if they opened fire at him or his marines, ditto for innocents passing across the Friendship Bridge.

Just wait a little longer, he thought. *Give us just a little time, then you can all go straight to Hell. Do not pass "Go," do not collect your fifty virgins on the way.*

It would be Butler's pleasure, introducing four more scum-bags to the Afterlife.

"Just take it nice and easy," Jack advised. "You see the uniforms and chopper."

"Leathernecks," Sara replied.

"Hey, did I ever tell you how they got that nickname?"

"Spare me!"

"Okay, then. You're spared."

They neared the Friendship Bridge on foot, under the watchful eye of Afghan border guards. One of the men in uniform met them and asked, "Americans?"

"I guess it shows," Jack said.

"I must examine your—"

The soldier never got as far as saying "papers," though. Or maybe Jack just missed it as a hissing, sizzling sound descended from the vast blue sky above them, joined by eerie whistling as some object moving too fast for the eye to follow plummeted to earth, somewhere between a half-mile and three-quarters of a mile along the river's southwest bank.

The Hellfire missile struck and detonated with a roar of dirty thunder, throwing off a fireball that ascended fifty feet or more into the air. Jack thought he saw a rag-doll figure in the midst of that explosion, soaring upward, losing broken limbs along the way.

Nearby, three other figures rose and bolted from ground zero, running for their lives. As usual, when running was essential to survival, they began too late and couldn't manage to attain escape velocity.

Another plunging comet hurtled down to impact on the

desert, and another fiery mushroom blossomed on the river's bank. The running men were there, and then they weren't, lost in a swirling storm of smoke and dust and flame.

Or maybe they had just been vaporized.

Their border guard was gaping at the damage, dark eyes shifting back and forth between the zone of desolation and the two Americans standing in front of him. At last, he waved them toward the bridge, saying, "Move on! Hurry!"

They passed him, heard him shouting something to the other guards in Uzbek, a derivative of Turkish with some Russian tossed in for variety. Jack reached for Sara's hand and saw her flinch a little, so he gave that up and broke into a jog.

"Last one aboard the Black Hawk," he advised her, "buys the first two rounds of beer."

EPILOGUE

Sar-e Pol Province, Afghanistan

Two nearly broken men sat in a tent, near the Sangcharak District's border with Samangan Province. The site was isolated by design, two bodyguards for each man circling around the tent with their Kalashnikovs.

"Sergeant Isani, it appears that you have come down in the world," Sediq Qayoumi.

"And you, as well," the ISI agent replied. "What should I call you now, Sediq? Do you have any rank at all within the Taliban these days?"

Nearly a month of hiding, dealing with recriminations for their failure, had elapsed since the Crusaders had escaped into Uzbekistan, leaving Isani's hit team scorched and scattered, nearly beyond recognition, on the Amu Darya's southern bank. Some might have been surprised these men were still alive. Instead of execution, though, their punishment—after demotion and a quasi-public shaming—was assignment to collaborate in a new venture aimed at NATO and America.

With luck, Isani thought, he might redeem himself, regain his former rank, and prove that his superiors were wrong in blaming him for unavoidable disaster. When that day came, he would be rid of Sediq Qayoumi for good.

"What is the brilliant plan this time?" Qayoumi asked Isani, not quite mocking him but coming close enough to set the Pakistani's teeth on edge.

"An army general from the Great Satan is expected in Kabul next week," Isani said, "beginning an inspection tour. I am assigned to welcome him and introduce him to *Jahannam*'s inferno."

"How does that affect me?" Sediq asked.

"He will be coming here, among his other stops, to Sar-e Pol. He must assess the province and its progress under the Americans."

Isani was not sure what that progress entailed. Nearly two decades since the Crusader invasion, 85 percent of households in the province had no decent drinking water. Only one in five births was attended by a skilled practitioner. Illiteracy... well, reports would make no difference, since few of the province inhabitants could read or write.

"And how am I supposed to help you?" Sediq asked.

"I need two martyrs, three at most, to greet this *lewanaya* with explosive vests and send him home in pieces. Send a message back to Washington that tells them we have not surrendered, and we never will."

"'We'?" Sadiq echoed. "Are you an Afghani now, Sergeant? Has the United States invaded Pakistan? If so, no one bothered to tell me."

"I'm referring to the Muslim world at large, as you well know."

"And so, by implication, placing Pakistan over the rest?"

Isani's sigh felt weary to him, must have sounded worse to his companion. "May we not, at long last, lay our animosity aside and serve the common good?"

"I *do* have access to the kind of youths you seek," Qayoumi granted. "Access, but no power of command, as I am sure you know by now. In fact, I am a hunted man myself."

"Spies and the drones. I know," Isani said. "All the more reason to strike back."

"Your plan is feasible, Sergeant," Sediq replied. He used the lower rank, Isani knew, to rub salt in the wound of Isani's demotion. "But I would be called upon for a donation to their families."

"I can arrange that, within reason. But—" Isani hesitated, lost his thought, and asked Sediq, "Do you hear that?"

"Hear what?"

A heartbeat later it was all too obvious. The warning whistle had become a howl as the approaching missile sped toward impact.

Sergeant Isani felt a muddled urge to laugh or cry, perhaps both at the same time.

Alas, there was no time to choose. There was not even time to pray.

A LOOK AT: THE LAST REFUGE
(CODY'S WAR BOOK FIVE)

FROM THE MODERN MASTER OF THE ACTION ADVENTURE M.I.A. HUNTER SERIES A NEW KIND OF MISSION...

Domestic terrorism. The worst kind.

A tiny US town on the Mexican border. Remote. A big day for this minuscule rural community. The president and First Lady are in town with their entourage to honor a deceased grand old man of the Party. A quick in-and-out visit to pay their respects and they'll be home in DC before dark.

Things go to hell when the crazed, homicidal Elkins clan hits town with their own bloody agenda. POTUS is taken hostage. Demands are made "or the executions will begin."

Back in Washinton, CIA field agent Sara Durell, satisfied in knowing her friend, Jack Cody, has at long last left government service, healed from the personal tragedies that earned him the nickname Suicide Cody. But Sara's world goes suddenly intense when once again she and Cody—this time separated by thousands of miles—must risk their lives to combat a brutal home front crisis.

AVAILABLE DECEMBER 2019

ABOUT THE AUTHOR

Stephen Mertz is an American fiction author who is best known for his mainstream thrillers and novels of suspense. His work covers a wide variety of styles from paranormal dark suspense (Night Wind and Devil Creek) to historical speculative thrillers (Blood Red Sun) and hardboiled noir (Fade to Tomorrow). Mertz is also a popular lecturer on the craft of writing and has appeared as a guest speaker before writer's groups and at universities.

Steve's writing output increased dramatically when he emerged as one of the country's most in-demand writers of adventure paperback novels, averaging four books per year for ten years. His work on Don Pendleton's Mack Bolan series is regarded by fans as some of the best in that series. He also created the Mark Stone: MIA Hunter and Cody's Army series, written under the pseudonyms Jack Buchanan and Jim Case respectively.

Stephen Mertz lives in the American Southwest, and he is always at work on a new book.

Find Stephen online: www.stephenmertz.com